G·A·A·Y

One hundred ways to love a beautiful loser

GW00778040

G·A·A·Y

One hundred ways to love a beautiful loser

JARLATH GREGORY

SITRIC BOOKS

First published 2005 by
SITRIC BOOKS
62–63 Sitric Road, Arbour Hill,
Dublin 7, Ireland
www.sitric.com

A CIP record for this title is available from
The British Library.

1 3 5 7 9 10 8 6 4 2

ISBN 1 903305 15 2

Set in 9 on 13.5 pt Slimbach with Conduit titling
Printed by MPG Books, Bodmin, Cornwall

The G.A.A. is the Gaelic Athletic Association.
G.A.Y. is a club night at the London Astoria.
Both are full of sweaty men.

1. Litter breeds everywhere (outside of the industrial estates)

You've got to fight to be fabulous. Sometimes it feels like trawling your arse out of bed isn't worth the sight of a sky filled up with towerblocks, but then love comes to slap your face and caress your balls all at once. It's fucking magic! I'm in love with love. It makes the paving-slabs glitter, it turns the litter into gold-dust, it even transforms snotty-nosed brats into wee angels. You walk around in the sort of good mood that makes people forget what a bitch you really are.

As our park's resident gay-boy, it's my duty to live life as an Abba song. Of course, sometimes it all goes wrong and you end up sounding like Aqua instead – *c'est la vie en rose*. I mean, that Tuesday I woke up completely out of love with my old crush, Cathal Woods, for the first time in, like, five years. What the hell was I meant to do? I'd used up every drama I could concoct from him and my mates – was it time to move on? I got to thinking how maybe I should fly to another city, or somewhere it never ever rains, but then I'd get bored of wearing tank-tops and drinking fruit cocktails all morning. So I went to get the stupidest haircut I could think of, just cos I needed the change. It was going to be the day that I first met Khalid Kashani. He changed the way I see my life. The soundtrack to my walking switched from plastic Europop to something always beautiful, and sometimes sad.

2. Anto sets the towerblocks alight

Khalid claims to be black and claims to be straight, neither of which seems true to me. His skin is golden, light, lighter than mine with the fake tan on. The skin beneath his eyes is smudged purple, as if he's wearing make-up, though it's natural. His hair and his eyes are a deep, rich brown, almost liquid, a colour that sublimates when the light defines him.

He's as bent as a banana.

Anyway. I didn't know that yet. All I knew was that it should have been a lush day, the kind where your hormones sing in haikus to every sexy bint in the street. I could see them from our fourth-floor window – skinheads, dreadlocks, bleached-tipped flicked fringes. On other days I could have found something cute in every one of them. I'll come clean – I wanted a new obsession.

I couldn't believe how colourless the world was without love. Even the sky was colourless, with clouds trailing through it like spunk in bathwater. Me and Dave did it in the bath once – well, three times at once if you know what I mean – but we were just fuck buddies, really. Good sex, no conversation. I knew it was over when he started speaking Klingon.

Back in the flat, the clutter of a Saturday morning sang out of tune. The telly and the radio were shouting for nothing. Kids barked outside, the dogs yapped, my family yawned and shoved around like inmates conscripted into some reality-TV gameshow. We were probably the reruns.

I scalded out the breakfast dishes and tried to escape without Ma nabbing me to help our Zak with his homework. He's fifteen, he should know enough by now to lie about it, but Ma's mad on education since she did that back-to-school scheme. My best mate Decko has a T-shirt that says 'School Spirit Still Haunts Me' – we know what it means.

Down the stairs, Darren was lying in a heap from last night. I patted his curly head on the way by, jumping the last flight of stairs in one go. Not bravado – just avoiding the shit smeared up it.

Cathal and his retard mates were kicking a bust football round the yard half-heartedly. It whacked off my perfect ass. I spun around – 'That's as close as *you're* ever getting!' – and Cathal glowed the dull red of cheap German wine.

The kids were chalking a yellow hopscotch grid on the tarmac. I skipped over it as Cathal yelled, 'It wasn't me, Anto!' to my backside. Whatever!

The last thing I saw on my way out of the yard was the curtain twitching in Mr McGinnity's ground-floor flat. His little half-smile cheered me up no end.

In the street, the flies around the bags of rubbish seemed to waltz in the air for my romantic notions. Times like this I want to set a trail of fireworks all the way from the street to our flats, throw a match to the lot, to see the multicoloured man-made stars explode and die, leaving only black tears dripping from the windows – cool.

3. School spirit still haunts me

Heterosexual thugs rule every boys' school. It was all very well being a cutesy drama fag who could step into Juliet's size 9s, but cutting a dash on the football field was *all*. Half-naked Neanderthal man had to chase wild boar to the death just to eat, while half-naked schoolkids have to kick a pig's bladder round a soggy pitch year in, year out, in the name of *recreation*. Sport is such a waste of evolution.

On the way into town, a delivery man dropped a whole tray full of salmon onto the pavement at Café King. If I was superstitious, I'd have seen it as some sort of sign. As it was, I ignored their dead staring eyes, flat on one side of their heads like wild-card jacks in a game of poker. I ignored their glittering skins and raw, tasty, gutted underbellies. I ignored their promise, and their warning, and as the man scooped the fish up from where the concrete ground its gritty kisses into alien flesh, I bounced on, oblivious, or so I thought, to the day unfolding around me.

In fact, I am superstitious, although I tell myself not to be so backwards, not to always face the future looking over my shoulder for ghosts.

4. Money springs from my heels like little wings

I never used to eat as a kid. It just meant too much to my parents. There I'd be, pushing round the muck on my plate, while they tried their best to cajole me into swallowing.

I didn't know what it meant not to be hungry, but I hugged my hunger to myself as a shield, and as a weapon, nursing it like a talisman, feeding it with glamorous dreams culled from TV. The small-screen stars, mere slivers of humanity that burned out in moments, pouted and vanished, were always my icons, and I wanted to be like them – ephemeral, two-dimensional, hyper-colourful and existing only in the most sexy or traumatic bits of life. *They* didn't have to eat; *they* didn't have to shit; *they* didn't fill time with small-talk, the news, washing their socks or worrying about money. Unfortunately, money is important when you haven't got any, and now I'm chasing the money that swims in shoals around Ireland, the tax-free kisses of culture, the allure of myself recreated as a brand, a commodity, a product. Way back when, I'd have been a rent-boy. Now, I'm in a boyband.

Louis Walsh is a god. Without talent, without charisma, without taste, he built a global empire from the unpromising mud of Irish youth. The best bit about his acts is that you needn't even know that they're Irish. He shrugged off history, culture and identity to the international sing-song of tills jingling with pre-teen pocket money. Oh, you might catch sight of the odd white horse in his admirably vacuous videos, but they're nothing compared to the white elephants of talent that he promotes. He's even clawed some respect from the music establishment by admitting *he's in it for the money*, which most of them secretly are – but then, who ever lost money by underestimating the public? He never claimed to be cool, he just follows his own bland-guy instinct and pushes the most malleable, inoffensive pap he can manufacture, like the musical equivalent of Pick'n'Mix sweets. My biggest ambition is to be Louis Walsh's Dolly Mixture.

Our manager wants us to be a bit cheekier than Louis Walsh's gang. It's more *now*. I can do cheeky. I could do *dirty* with those two lookalikes out of Busted and McFly, if they'd let me. But even that cheekiness is rehearsed – it's about having messy-but-clean hair and pretending you've got a four-bottles-of-beer buzz going on, *all the time*.

I crave that empty lifestyle, and never having to feel another true and tired emotion.

So I admit, I'm confused about love. Sometimes it feels like it's all I ever do, fall for the wrong guy, nurture that insatiable hunger for my own protection from reality. Then sometimes when I think that I've never known love at all, that infatuation conquers me with just the right smile at the right time – Bang! – and I've shot myself in the foot again.

I aspire to be the streamlined dream of cyborgs, to sex as electricity, to desires satisfied as easily as charging up your mobile phone. But love is my Achilles' heel, and pain reminds you you're alive – right?

5. Flawless

A haircut is a chore. I mean, the scruffy look works if you wear the sort of clothes that mismatch in various shades of drab, but I prefer to be magazine-fresh. Having to walk and sweat and talk with your mouth full spoils the effect, but wouldn't you rather be remembered for a flawless pose? Mentally, we're all on the catwalk. If you're not, then you're not on my planet. You probably have more body hair than actual clothes.

Getting a haircut is a reminder of the impossibility of perfection. It's admitting that your head goes through that in-between stage of unshaggability. If I ever wanted to grow my hair I'd have to switch off my life for a couple of months, stay indoors and turn all the mirrors to the wall. I'd probably turn lesbian with worthiness.

An absolute mannequin with the best make-up I'd seen all morning shoved a flyer in my hand. I smiled back at her – her lips were so glossy they seemed to simply slide apart like grinning automatic doors – and wondered if I could copy her look onto Cathy for her next photoshoot. I didn't even look at the ad until I'd tallied all the ammo I'd need for that face, but when I did, I stopped dead. I turned red. I went apeshit.

I flung myself around, stormed through the grey hordes of stragglers till I saw Ms Mannequin's face shine in mine.

Livid!

'Do I look,' I fumed, 'like the sort of guy who'd go to a *lap-dancing* club?'

Her glossy lips failed her.

'Do I *look* heterosexual?'

Her eyes hit the windscreen with a splat.

'Would I spend so much money looking *fabulous* if I wanted to pass as *straight*?'

I flung her tits-and-ass flyer at her feet. The poor girl bawled. She wept a fucking torrent, and the old dears around us tut-tutted as if we'd just had a lovers' tiff. .

'S-sorry,' she sniffed.

I'm not completely heartless, much as I'd like to be. Her tears ripped me right off the cover of *Attitude* and back into the grimy exhausted air of Dublin city.

'Oh here, don't cry,' I sighed. She snuffled some more and I patted her shoulder. She wiped her nose with the back of her hand, and, as she looked into my face, I realized how lovely her eyes were. It was a revelation.

'Where the hell did you get that mascara?' I asked, amazed. 'It hasn't even *clumped*.'

6. I am a gay cliché

I've always been a total faggot. I played with my sisters' Barbie dolls and did my best to dress my Action Man in her clothes. Ma tried to compromise by buying me a short-haired sailor Sindy – talk about exacerbating gender confusion. I fantasized about being Cinderella, and out-diva'ed the girls when it came to raiding Ma's make-up bag and dancing round to *Top of the Pops*. You get the picture. I'm just one of those boys who sprang from the womb in a prom dress.

Listen to me. 'Prom dress'. Tacky American teen shows are so gay!

The best bit is, I was the most radical little queer you could've met. I flaunted my girliness with ever-batting eyelashes, exaggerated it by bleaching my hair since the age of nine, and spent my school years rehearsing for the future fame I knew I would achieve. When you've got the guts to be famous in your own postcode area, you know you can take on the world. My finest hour was winning the 'Best Actress' award in an All-Ireland school drama festival.

It wasn't all sunlight and roses though – every budding drag queen needs her tragedy. Mine is epic. The roots go much deeper than an alcoholic ma or a bad daddy, or even smoking crack while skipping gym class. Any of that would have *helped* when I was playing Truth or Dare with the other attention-seeking wannabes.

OK.

Deep breath.

My parents are …

Sporty.

G.A.A. sporty.

Doesn't sound too bad, does it, once you say it out loud? But it was crippling at the time. There were always hordes of guys knocking on the front door, ringing about training times, wondering if Da could squeeze in an extra fitness program at the weekend. Worse still, all the bijou dykettes coming round to bash up my ankles with their camogie sticks while Ma put on her other tracksuit. Have you any idea? A football coach, one of those natural enemies of the gay child, for a *da*. And a camogie coach, a gung-ho, outdoorsy *butch* for a ma. I lived in fear that Duane or Kevo might come round to practise our routines and find a pack of apes in the local colours clogging up our dancefloor – namely, our fourth-floor steps.

Just don't go thinking this is some sort of confessional. I'm way over the Catholic thing.

7. Turning blond beneath his gaze

I planned my day while I sat in the barber's chair. I probably chatted away the whole time, without listening to a word my barber said. So what? No one truly fabulous needs to listen during a conversation.

The haircut was easy – a number one all over, except for a Mohican that ran from the nape of my neck to exactly halfway up the top of my skull. It was deadly. I made such a cute little punk! My manager would freak, but I'm not listening until she evolves into Louis.

I texted Cathy as the bleach sucked dry my roots.

> abc   339/1
> Found a fab new
> mascara, can't
> wait to paint ur
> face! Wanna
> meet 4 kaw-fee
> & discuss world
> poverty? Or
> maybe new
> shoes?!
>   Options

It takes brains to be this dumb. To maintain the façade that your life is so much fun while secretly you're wondering when your real life will start to make sense.

I love pop. Its appeal lies as much in its throwaway, use-once-and-destroy aesthetic as in its veneer of inauthenticity. Pop is real. True music-lovers know that behind the slap and tickle, pop is a hard graft and an unforgiving discipline. Sure, you've got to look good, stick to the script and hope the media take the bait. But the hooks have to bypass your brain and aim straight for the heart, and you just can't fake sex appeal. As any gay man will tell you, style *is* substance.

An Asian-y looking guy caught my eye in the mirror. He was getting his hair cropped and messed up. He grinned slyly at me, just for a second, before his barber flipped his face away with light fingertips.

'How's the length, sir?'

'Yeah, choppy, that's great.' His accent was soft South London.

'Rico,' the hairdresser proclaimed, 'I would *die* for a hot chocolate!'

My barber protested. 'I have to keep an eye on this gentleman's roots. I can't have his scalp getting scalded and flaking on his *lovely* T-shirt. Did you get that in Flip?'

'Yeah, but you have to look in the girls' section –'

'Oh, I *know*. They're much more fitted –'

'Hot chocolate, Rico?!' You could totally hear the punctuation.

My barber bristled, but the Londoner broke the tension.

'I'll get it,' he said.

'No, no –'

'There's no need –'

Querulous hands flew, flashing scissors.

'It's cool. I want to.'

'It might just save my scalp,' I chimed in. I was rewarded with a wink in the mirror.

Flummoxed, the barbers shrugged at each other, warily. The Londoner stood up. 'Will I leave my watch here? Till I get back?'

'No … I trust you.'

'Do you take sugar in your hot chocolate?'

'No sugar. But. Eh. Two marshmallows?'

'OK. Back in a sec – what's your name?'

'Ben.'

'I'm Khalid. Back in a sec, Ben.'

They shook hands, and Ben broke into a smile.

'Khalid?'

'Yeah?'

'You know you've still only had half a haircut?'

Khalid glanced in the mirror and ran a hand through his asymmetrical hair.

'It's kind of funky. I won't be long.'

'Don't you want to, eh, take off the cape before you go?'

'Nah. Makes me feel like a superhero.'

Then Khalid sauntered out the door, and the three of us sighed like schoolgirls.

My phone chirped.

**Not sure about
your make up
choices nearly
as bad as your
taste in men !
Simons Place 4
lunch at 1 ish ? C
xox
Options**

Khalid came back with two hot chocolates, one for Ben and one for Rico. I caught his eye a couple of times, though I didn't mean to, and when he left with both Ben and Rico's numbers he didn't look back at all.

Within half an hour my hair shone in golden spikes, like rays of sunlight erupting from my brain.

8. Bittersweet drug

'We learned such a lot about the vagina this week,' Cathy enthused. 'Did you know –'

'Probably not –'

'– that all its juices and squeezy muscles make it perfect for sucking in the penis and giving pleasure to the male and female simultaneously? Isn't that marvellous?'

'What a load of nonsense. I get much more pleasure from shoving my cock up someone's arse.'

'No you don't. Because the anal passage isn't *meant* for drawing in – oh, obviously, you can do it if you want, that's *fine* –' Cathy added, with hasty and spurious political correctness, '– but it's got harder walls much better equipped for *expelling*. It says so in the medical books.'

'Obviously written by a heterosexual. I saw my first vagina last week when some yoke at work was looking up Internet porn. She was shoving a bright green dildo up her. I nearly puked at the sight of her bits.'

'Oh, I don't know,' Cathy mused. 'I'm sure vaginas are much prettier than penises. Oh dear, was that a lesbian moment?'

We all have to be patient about Cathy's 'lesbian moments'. They seem to occupy about, oh, sixty seconds per minute.

'And you know, although the issue of anal sex was addressed during class –'

'By a heterosexual non-practiser of the gentle art of buggery –'

'– they never mentioned performing, you know, oral sex on a woman.' Cathy lapped up the foam on her cappuccino and collapsed in giggles.

I really didn't want to know why.

'Anyway,' I said, 'medical books have to pretend that we're here for the sole purpose of breeding. Fabulous people like me are here to show all you duty-bound breeders how much fun you're missing. I really have no intention of poking round anyone's vagina, Cathy, although I'm sure yours is just peachy.'

'Nipples!' said Cathy. By now, some worried habitués of Simon's Place were staring.

'What?'

'I've always thought peachy was a nice colour for nipples. Nice pinky, peachy nipples, much more feminine than brown nipples, you know?'

'No,' I said.

'Any men?'

'Nope. I'm over Cathal though. I suppose that's progress.'

'How come?'

'I don't know. I just woke up this morning with a rush of blood to the head, thinking it was time for something new. Hence the hair.'

'I'm glad. I never liked Cathal anyway. He's such a knacker.'

'Cathy!'

'What?'

'*I'm* a knacker!'

'Don't be silly, Anto,' Cathy said, patting my arm. 'You're *gay*. It's a completely different social niche.'

'Well, I'm a gay knacker then.'

'Hmmm. Whatever you are, you're much too good for Cathal. Besides, your babies would be redheads.'

'Cathy, darling,' I drawled, 'I think you should read your medical books more *carefully.*'

I watched the marshmallows, one white, one pink, melt in the dregs of bittersweet hot chocolate. Swirling them into a heart-shaped gooey mess, I drank the lot.

9. Moments

If life is lived in moments, how many moments do we get in one lifetime? This is the sort of shit I worry myself with when I'm supposed to be acting frivolous and not seeing any of the fragmentary beauty around me.

I live my life as if on camera, as if a vast invisible audience is tuned into my every move. I'm constantly switched on, watching stories and situations unfold according to the wider script, until multinationals are ready to endorse me, or, more profitably, the *idea* of me … but perfect movie moments are rare. When they happen, when something bizarre or beautiful strays across your path, you have to seize upon it, burn it into place in your brain. You have to capture that moment and store it away as a reminder that, sometimes, life seems as elegantly designed as Disney would have us believe.

10. I can't resist a movie moment

Dublin stinks. The streets are always streaming with piss and puke from the night before. The whiff of processed cheese permeates Grafton Street, as if sewer rats are boiling up vast vats of smegma underground. It isn't romantic. Yet the buzz of tourists and lunchtime loungers always gets my spirits up. The pubs are never empty. People chatter and holler, and you can guarantee the most idle stroll around town will mean bumping into someone you know.

'Anto!'

'Jennifer!'

My younger sister Jennifer has a thing for camp men. Every time she gets a new boyfriend, we hear how nice, cute, clean, funny and well dressed he is – and he's always *such a good dancer*. Then she takes him home, and we're all waiting to hear just how gay his voice is. So when I saw her standing in brand-new boots at the gates of Trinity, I suspected she might be meeting some boy who'd appreciate swanky footwear.

'You're in time to meet my new man!'

'I'll shake his hand and see if he's limp-wristed.'

'He's *definitely* straight this time – he plays football. He's a cutie, but I don't know what Ma would say!'

'Why?'

'Here he is!'

That was why. The first thing I saw was his skin. The second thing I saw was *him*.

Khalid, the superhero of the Barber Room, Captain Hot Chocolate himself, strolled through Trinity Front Arch with his new haircut gleaming in the sudden flush of sunshine. It was one of those moments. As he put his arm around my beaming sister, he pressed his finger to his lips in a silent 'ssshhh'.

Love, or something like it, scattered like pollen. I sneezed.

11. Warning: Smoking can seriously damage your heart

'Sweetie,' Terry decried, 'what is it about you and straight men?'

'He doesn't sound very straight,' Decko mused. 'Getting hairdressers' numbers?'

'I don't *have* a thing for straight men,' I protested. 'They're always closet cases.'

'Sweetie, that's worse. They've got *issues.*'

'And we say *no* to issues, and *no* to baggage,' Decko reminded me.

I sighed. You have to be constantly vigilant against a façade of masculinity, or a fear of intimacy, or his ex-boyfriend, or religion – just some of the most common forms of issues and baggage being lumbered around. Mostly, those weighed down don't realize what they're carrying. It's much more fabulous to travel light.

'Anyway, he's dating your sister.'

'That didn't stop him with Adam.'

'I only snogged Adam once! And it's not like we could have taken it further, I mean, Jennifer was on his lap at the time.'

'Yeah, *that* makes it OK.'

'And whatever happened to Tommy Riordan?'

'He's still engaged. I think he's still cross-country running too. You know, his time must have improved so much when I quit the team.'

'And we used to wonder why he seemed so drained and always came second last.'

'Quick, Anto! Make a joke about who came first!'

'Oh, shut up.'

'And then there was James Murphy.'

'That was romantic,' I said. 'It was at that party in Belfast –'

'Sweetie, I *know*. My sister was there and absolutely *started* the rumour that James kissed Decko that very night!'

'What? Me?'

'Sweetie, she knew it was *one* of the boyband bum-bandits.'

'Yeah, but he's got fat since then,' Decko huffed.

'We were on the front porch,' I continued, 'Emily and Deedee were raging I invited him, cos they'd both been with him before. He left the girlfriend at home and I left my fella inside – he was chatting up Cathy –'

'No!'

'Yeah, he said afterwards he really fancied her.'

'But sweetie, does she look like a man?'

'Well, Rock does like androgynous lesbians.'

'Cathy's beautiful.'

'Is she boyish, though?'

'I don't think so. He fancies her anyway, and I was alone with James. I sat on the pillar at the gate, and Naomi yelled, "Oh for fuck's sake, just snog him!" Then she stormed off to tell Rock I was cheating on him. After we kissed, he said, "Could you do that again – and not bite my tongue off?" But all the stars were out –'

'Yeah, yeah.'

'– and after we kissed more gently, all he could say was, "You're my first ..." then all these yobbos walked past sniggering and he tried to be all laddy and pally with them. You've got to decide whose side you're on, you know?'

'He'll marry her.'

'No, he dumped her already –'

It might seem that I'm really into bi-curious guys, but in my defence, they're more into me. Maybe it's cos they can kid themselves I'm practically a girl. Later that night, a guy who'd been hanging around as Terry, Decko and I air-kissed our goodbyes started to follow me home.

'Have you got a light?'

'Yeah, sure.' I gave him my packet of matches. 'Keep them.'

I walked on, but he kept pace as he lit up. He studied the packet of matches before pocketing them.

'The Front Lounge?'

'Yep. Ever been?'

'Aye, once.'

'It's cool.'

'It's alright. I didn't stay long. You from round here?'

'Ish. Yeah. You?'

'Tipperary.'

I looked at him sideways, smoking in profile. He had a cute nose and carefully groomed facial hair. Then a crowd of his mates materialized, shouting 'Johnny!' and I slipped on ahead, wondering what might have happened next.

Town was busy enough, with taxis crawling between the lurch-legged couples and sour streams of bodily fluids. The sky was dark but overcast, like velvet rubbed the wrong way. I shoved my hands deeper into my pockets and smelled chips frying, heard jocular foreign voices jibing each other.

Footsteps.

I tensed.

'Hi! Front Lounger!'

'Hey, Johnny.'

'Them were my mates. Bit of bother. Where are you going?'

'Home.'

'Come here.'

'Yeah, right.'

'Come on.'

'So you can chop me up into little pieces?'

'No! Come on.'

He was urgent. I was curious. I followed him down a well-lit side street. Noise faded to the rustle of dying leaves.

'What's your name?'

'Anto. Nice of you to ask.'

We pressed ourselves against a wall by tall iron gates. Newish apartments squared their shoulders and stared blankly over our heads. We kissed, and Johnny poured his urgency through me.

'Hey!'

His hands went straight down my jeans.

'There's CCTV watching us.'

'We'll go somewhere else.'

'We can go to my place.'

'We can't share a bed – that's too gay.'

'Are you sure?'

'Yeah.'

'Let's find somewhere in from the road then.'

Surprisingly, he took my hand. We clambered over the kerbside and into the dark doorway of someone's semi-detached home. We were semi-detached ourselves, fumbling, excited, too quickly, and –

'Have you done that before?'

'Un-hunh.'

'Jesus, you're a natural! Hey, don't stop –'

'I want you to fuck me.'

'No way!'

'Please.' He bent over, loosening his belt. A trio of shiny girls fell past and didn't even notice.

'No way, it's not safe. Jesus. You never fuck without a condom.'

'I'll fuck you then.'

'I don't know where you've been!'

'Please. Come on.'

'Come home.'

'Fuck me. I need to see what it's like.'

He dropped his pants. It was funny – almost.

'I'll do it just for a minute then. I won't cum.'

He did the usual groaning as I pushed myself inside. He seemed to like it, but I pulled out pretty quickly. He sank to the ground.

'Suck my cock,' he said.

'Suck mine,' I said.

'After where it's been?'

We both laughed, briefly. He took my hand, stood up, quickly let go again.

'I'm a brickie,' he said.

'Right.'

'I live with all these lads. They wouldn't understand … what do you do?'

'Telesales.'

He didn't answer, just buckled himself up again, tucked in his Ben Sherman shirt.

'Don't you want to suck my cock?' He seemed a little hurt that I didn't.

'Can't your girlfriend do that?'

'Yeah.' He spat. 'I definitely prefer girls anyway. Bye.'

'Bye.'

He walked off with his head held high.

I stood in some stranger's garden with my mickey hanging out.

'Good luck!' I called after him.

'Yeah. If you see me around, you don't know me!'

Which was fair enough. I might not recognize him in daylight anyway.

I texted Decko and Terry on my way home.

```
abc              383/1
Just copped a BJ
off sum str8
fella. U may call
me Anto
'Ladyboy'
Broderick!
        Options
```

    I lit up a celebratory cigarette with my lighter. I only carry extra matches for sexy people.

12. The language of sex

The language of sex is the language of loss. We become divisible, seeking to leave something of ourselves in others. We offer the other a share of our stories, and become written into the story of their lives in return.

What we leave behind is fluid, yet to settle and be subsumed, transformed into a manageable anecdote that finds a home amid the rhythm we impose upon our histories.

We make up our lives as we go along. We come. We go.

13. The subtle play of cigarettes on skin

That guy Johnny was no big deal. Maybe I went with him because I was bored, maybe because I was over Cathal, maybe because he asked, maybe because I knew it was his first time, maybe because he had a cute nose, maybe because we'd been talking about me and my straight men and I thought it would be funny. It doesn't really matter. I wonder how much of a big deal it was to Johnny – but after all, I could have been any anonymous faggot, so it isn't my problem. It's like the opposite of being gay-bashed. I didn't take it personally.

To me, sex isn't that important. It's fun, it's something to talk about, and it's inaccurate to think that because I'm out, because I openly identify myself as a gay man, it follows that I define my life in terms of sex. All my life, other people have defined me according to my behaviour – other people insist I'm different, not me. To be out is to say that love and sex are natural, are no more complicated than they should be, are happening no matter how someone else wants to suppress you. Maybe it's easier for me because I've always been seen as different.

I want to live my life to show other people it's not so tough. I want Cathal to see that I'm happy, that it's cool, but then I roll home at 3 a.m. and he's smoking his brains out on the wall, surrounded by cans and broken bottles.

'Howaya, Anto?'

'I'm alright. How're you?'

'I'm gonna be alright … inside.'

'Come on then.'

He accepted my hand and slid off the wall. He slowly released my fingers, shook himself.

'Have you got a light?'

'Sure.'

He cupped his hands around mine as I fired up his cigarette. His eyes, his face, glowed like cinnamon. He slowly unfolded his hands. I turned to home.

He didn't move.

'You should watch it, Anto.'

'Should I? Why?'

'People round here. I'm just saying. You know why.'

I looked back. 'You know, you're OK when those cunts aren't around.'

He looked to the ground. He scuffed his trainers amongst cigarette butts and cellophane.

''Night,' I said, but he didn't answer.

I walked on home, looking out of every stairwell window between Cathal and the fourth floor, seeing his face stay stuck to the ground, his foot scuffing at nothing much, his cigarette dying unheeded between his short, rough fingers.

14. Of such things our youth is dreamt

I'd lied to Johnny about coming back to mine. I share bunk beds with my little brother Zak. I lay awake remembering how I'd been at Zak's age.

Being fifteen.

'I love you too, Anto,' Cathal had said for no reason other than he meant it. He was dressing straight out of the showers, and all the boys were roundabout.

'Yeah, I know,' I'd said quietly, to myself really, with my shaved head and black jeans, going through a phase of trying to be a man, although I am one.

I think we both meant it, then. I'd fallen in love with him one week before, ever since I came in out of the rain, last off the pitch cos Da made me hunt for lost balls, water just pure dripping off my face. Finding him standing there in front of me, his red hair burning through the rain, his eyes inviting mischief. I'd pushed past him roughly. Naked, I'd looked everywhere but back at Cathal's pretty face, his loose-hanging arms, his ready smile. Back then, I'd thought I would never be ready.

I had lain in the same bed that night five years ago and prayed not to be gay. It must have been the first time I acknowledged to myself that I wasn't just 'different', whatever that meant. I had a name. I had several. You could learn them from graffiti in toilets or on the back of vans, or from kids in a playground who all seemed to know my secret years before I did.

I quit football sometime that month, devastated that all the slurs people threw at me were true. It took me a while to recapture that 'fuck you' attitude of the carefree child I'd been. I guess I'm still working on it.

In bed, in the dark, I raised my palm and pressed it to the ceiling. As usual, I tried to push through, to feel solidity crumble, will it to crash around my prone and restless body. When had Cathal become so *weary*?

A scrabble in the corner. A squeak. I yelped.

'Ssshhh!' Zak said, prodding me from the bottom bunk. 'It's my mouse!'

'It's not *your* fucking mou –'

'Shut up!' Zak's torch-beam froze the marauding mouse in its glare. 'I want to see what it does next!'

15. Orchestral silence and the morning

'Ma, we've got mice in the house. Zak wants to keep them and train them and start a mini-circus.'

'I'll get the traps out later.'

'Yuk! That'll mean little dead bodies in my bedroom!'

'Listen to you. Squeamish, and the age of him. Are you a man or a – oh, haha! Man or mouse! Haha!'

'Yeah, Ma, whatever.'

'Hahaha!'

'Bye, Ma.'

'Oh, that's a good one ...'

It was one more morning. I was wearing my gay uniform: flared jeans (girls'), retro T-shirt (fitted), bright trainers (girlie, but size 9), shiny new hair, perky attitude, the promise of gossip. I met Decko at the top of the road, lit up, and we walked towards work – real work that is, not singing lessons.

'So, tell us about last night's rudeness!'

'Oh god, he was such a minger!'

'Yeah?'

'He had facial hair.'

'Ugh.'

'Quite cool facial hair though. Sideburns. They sort of squared up his jawline.'

'Ah.'

'But he had such a dinky little nose, I couldn't refuse.'

'So he came onto you?'

'Absolutely.'

'And did he, er, *perform*?'

'Yep.'

'Ten extra points to you!'

'He had a girlfriend, too.'

'Twenty extra points!'

'Just doing my duty for the bi-curious.'

'So noble. So selfless.'

'Thank you.'

We passed stunted terraced housing with struggling gardens and the odd triumphant 'SOLD!' sign in the window. Socialist graffiti yelled at us from dodgy alleyways. We took a short cut through the shoulder-high rushes that flourish by the river, which chokes on its own silt and trickles like a kidney-dialysis machine. We saw no one else. The Industrial Estate gleamed on the horizon, always unreal no matter how many mornings we arrived there. It is hungry for dreams, and once you set foot on its perfectly swept gravel, with its strategically beautiful and lifeless ponds, time stands still. The buildings are testament to the soul-consuming gulf that money furnishes, with glass, with aluminium, with invisible rooftops, and so many mirrored windows – blank, reflecting only the sky and yourself – an unrecognizable glint in the eye of the face of conglomeration.

We clocked in, counting down the minutes until we could unhook our faces again.

16. Being in the band

Even as we sit over coffee, we're rehearsing dance moves. When we answer our phones, our cut-and-spliced lyrics bounce like Lotto numbers through our brains. The birds that flicker round the regular treetops sing our praises. The keyboards clatter in a backing rhythm to our Technicolor lives, and we shimmy to the water dispenser and back, light refracting off our buttons and our eyes. Our muscles synchronize. We slide into place as easily as drugs suffuse the blood, and every movement is a lubricated kiss, every word a hook that sticks to your lips, reels you in, and you can't help but dance to our tunes.

The lyrics are easy. It's all about you, me, a sunny day and a climbing, killer chorus that kids can sing the first time. What you can't fake is us: when we smile, we mean it; when we laugh, we feel it; when we tell you we love you, we need you, it's true. We want you to buy us, and learn how to always be happy too.

17. Everyone in my phone

Ally   Photographer. Cool.

Amy   From the North. Met her in The Kremlin. The North is grim.

Andrew   Dance tutor from way back when. Has girlfriends. Is a total queen whoever he sleeps with.

Anto   First boyfriend. Having same name caused much amusement, for three seconds. Only wears black. We never did anything rude, which is a shame. He's still gorgeous – sigh!

Astrid   Manager. It's just business.

Astrid (Home)   For when she's too hungover to get out of bed.

Barbie   Short for Barbara. Glam, should have a string of fellas, never does. Possible wife in a parallel universe?

Benji   We did a movie together once. Cool.

Brendan   No luck with men. Good for lunch and a gossip.

Brendan G.D.   Oh yeah, that Brendan. We used to work together. Forgot about him.

Brian   Moved to London. Mean to visit, never do.

Casey   Friend of a friend. Cool. Will never ring her.

Cathy   Another Med student (and don't you forget it!). Part-time model. Full-time closet case. We met at a Coming Out workshop. She said she was there because her boyfriend was gay.

Christine   We met in Transition Year and like to get pissed together. Way-hey!

Ciara   Schoolchum. Bump into her now and then. She has a perfect life and will most likely forge a career with the disabled, in Sweden.

Clint   Drinking buddy. Except he doesn't drink.

Connor   Med student. Used to slice his arms up over his ex. Has a new man now and wears Prada.

Cory   We were meant to meet somewhere once for some reason. Never did. I quite fancy his mate though, so I kept his number. Heh heh!

Credit Balance *174*

Customer Care

Damo   Model.

Daniel   Other guy in the band. He's a natural. He's the best. If anyone makes it, he should. We've started to see more of him outside of rehearsals, so maybe he'll become part of the story. Maybe he won't.

Dave   Ex.

David   Ex.

Davidé   Foreign bloke. Italy or Spain or somewhere. Not out to parents – running away? Has a hairy chest and wears a gold chain.

Decko   Mates since dance classes in Transition Year. We both work in Directory Enquiries and want to make it big with my boyband. I mean, our boyband.

Diggory   Bi-curious workmate. Haven't snogged him yet.

Donald   Fellow dancer and showbiz wannabe. Works in a bank. Never goes by this, his real name, which is why I revel in calling him by it.

Ferdy   Always either pissed or broke. Always snog him when drunk. Oops!

Derek   Musician. Cool. Has seven ex-girlfriends and one serious boyfriend (this week).

Domino's Pizza

Dozer   Schoolchum. Was a freak, so I liked him.

Eddie   I'm not sure which Eddie this is. Either the guy who worked in a sauna and wrote poetry, or the guy who goes to saunas and writes articles. Hmmm.

Eddy   Bleach-blond. Likes lesbian music and skincare products. Meet him at parties a lot.

Eddy X   Throws great parties, which the other Eddie attends. No idea what he does – business? Something in a suit. Perhaps he works in a bank like everybody else. Has four cats and a dog.

Emily   Learned about life from *Dynasty*. Could've been a rich divorcée in previous life.

Eoin   Journalist.

Fearghal   Used to have coffee with him, before he married his fella. Wears jumpers.

Felicity   Old-school lesbian. Handy with a Black & Decker.

Four Springs   Record Company.

Frances   In Australia this year.

Gerda   Journalist.

Greta   I think Cathy fancies her.

Helena   Where has Helena disappeared to?

Int Customer Care

Izzy   Works in a bank. Cool.

Jennifer   First-year English student. Ma and Da are dead proud. Has an apartment in town and a chronic fascination with gay men. At this point, still dating Khalid, whose number I do not have. Yet.

Jordan   I think he might be dead. Don't want to erase his number, in case that makes it true.

Katy   Aunt.

Kevin   Rock's boyfriend. Malaysian, can't spell his real name.

Leonora   Met her at a wedding. Texted her randomly while pissed once. We conversed until I ran out of credit.

Liamo   Publicist.

Lilith   Used to be in a band together. Now she has a husband and a mortgage. Which is a happy ending, I suppose.

Lou   Drama student. Cool.

Mairéad   Singer. Likes a drink or ten. Threw up in Jennifer's sink one memorable morning, while friend-of-a-friend prepared for her first job interview. Suzie scrubbed the sink clean ... the first time. Come to think of it, haven't seen her since.

Mandy   Moved to London. Will soon breed.

Mario, Belgium   Singer. Another player of the fame game.

Mario, Ireland   He stays here every so often and has a bevy of interesting friends.

Mary   Ma.

Mully   Decko's boyfriend. Feline. Bogger.

Naomi   Doing law. We hope she'll bail us out when she's rich.

Net Café   Where Mully works. We get freebies. Yay!

Ollie   Da.

Owen   Young man about town. The drag queens' favourite. Into drugs, self-improvement and philosophy.

Packy   Used to work together. Will never call him either.

Pam   Journalist.

Paul   Can never remember what he does. Likes a bitch, so we get on. Out since fifteen, has eight-year boyfriend. Another party person.

Paulie   Style queen.

Pauly   Queen.

Rachel Rath   Actress. Her family deserves a sitcom.

Randy   Wants to be a writer. Likes older gentlemen.

Ricardo   Fashionista. Well, works in a clothes shop. Has a nice piercing and wants to study film.

Robster   Son of a vicar, or something. Staunch atheist. Looks like an ex of mine whose number I deleted.

Rock   Ex. Also works in a bank. Bankers are the new proletariat and, of course, they don't even know it. Wears too much beige. My mission in life is to overhaul his wardrobe, his image, his shag-gability. He needs to look more like – me.

Róisín   Professional lesbian. Cool.

Roger   In media. Borrows other people's clothes.

RTG Talkback

Sally   Manager at work. Formidably efficient. Buys us biscuits and remembers everybody's quirks.

Sorcha   Hippy-chick. Cool.

Stina   Journalist.

Suzie   Our blondest cousin. Worrying addiction to American teen shows and Bon Jovi.

Terry   Works in a bank and drinks gin and tonic. Sometimes drinks it at home, with a real lime.

Voicemail

Victor   Geek chic web designer. Had a bit of a will-we-won't-we going on. Didn't. Cool.

Zak   Youngest sibling. Spoiled rotten, of course. Doesn't drink, anti-drugs, pro-profit, laid back. Thinks we're all a mess. Scarily aware of opportunities in corporate finance.

18. Who do you smell of?

I love finishing expensive toiletry products just so I can go and buy some more. It's great! I always try something new. Sometimes I'm lured by the jazziest packaging, other times I can't resist how fresh and green a shower gel looks, and when in doubt, I buy the whole range of something basic and strategically marketed: deodorant, shower gel, exfoliating gel, toner, moisturizer, shampoo, conditioner, hair gel, hair wax, shaving gel, shaving balm, in cool and complementary colour combinations. The only thing you don't buy from the range is your aftershave scent – that has to be consistently *you*. Sure, it's thousands of other people too, but it's comforting to know that I belong to an internationally identifiable target market. It's the first step in escaping my parents' lives. I refuse to turn into my parents. I refuse to breed.

Isn't it cool that other people dedicate their lives to suggesting how you smell? It's just one less thing for us all to worry about. I wouldn't say that advertising *works* on me – but if I haven't heard of a product, then it can't be much use, because it doesn't sell, and it can't afford to promote itself properly. So a lack of advertising certainly doesn't work, you know? And if a product is good but underestimates me, the consumer, by trying to get away with substandard advertising that insults my intelligence, then it doesn't deserve my money or my loyalty. It doesn't deserve my lending it credibility with my cash.

19. Going out

The best bit about going out is getting ready. The expectation! Helping Cathy experiment with more daring make-up (lesbians!), trying to look groomed without becoming a hairdresser from Dundalk, drinking just enough to put a sparkle on the lights of Centra as we teeter to the bus-stop.

Decko and Mully are snuggling together for warmth, drunk enough not to care who might see them, and no one passes any remarks – which is both cool and something my da would not believe. I think the fear of stigma is greater than stigma itself.

Beep BEEP Beep! Beep BEEP Beep!

Beep BEEP Beep! Beep BEEP Beep!

> **Me& Khalid**
> **drunky all read**
> **y. C yis in7ide x**
> **Jen**
> **Options**

A taxi pulls out in front of a bus, sending both of them skidding arse-ways across the road. Brakes and women squeal. Men emerge from the caverns of their robo-dinosaurs and square up, rut in the middle of the road. Oil, like blood, catches starlight. We breathe in the hormones and leaded petrol emissions that float on the air, say *fuck it*, and walk to the club with shining eyes and fizzy tongues.

20. Mates

I'd forgotten how minging straight clubs are. The boys are leery and the girls are desperate, and when I saw the girls made-up to the max and batting their heavy-lidded eyes at groups of fellas drooling over their scanty, glittered, skin-tight clothes, I wondered, *Is that what we look like in The George?*

We made our way through the crowd. There was actually a smoke-machine, replicating that pre-smoking-ban atmosphere. Beer for the boys and vodka for the ladies – we were all a little cliché. The music was OK. The crowd was too tightly packed, we sweated lightly just getting to the bar. I'd also forgotten how show-offy and loud groups of straight guys can be. Decko and I raised our eyebrows at each other, laughing telepathically at how yuk and school-like the situation seemed.

Jennifer found us and dragged us to the dancefloor where Khalid was moving stiffly to the stupid tune. When he picked me up and spun me like a bride in the middle of the floor, I kissed his cheek and he grinned like he'd scored a goal in the trials for his new club team. Jennifer smiled too, and it seemed to me, even as my head swam beneath the swirling eyes of the mirror ball, that she was giving us her blessing.

'I really admire your hair, Anto!' Khalid said.

I knew we were going to get on.

21. The shrinking feeling of global guilt

I don't want to know about suffering and war. Trying not to feel bored and unknown is about the only level of reality I can deal with. Distracting myself with stuff *works*, up to a point. Is doing my best not to let world-wide catastrophe get in the way of my kicks inhuman? Or is it a measure of my humanity that, if I'm lucky enough to live relatively untroubled, I should do my best to keep happy? Don't I owe that much to the people who never get the chance?

And if I get wiped out in an instant, why should I care for what I'll never regret? Believing in a finite life is not a death sentence. It's freedom. It's a spur on to do everything I want to do starting *now*.

Mornings kill me with their fresh-painted newness, every day. I think I want to die while I'm awake, just because it's the last chance I'll ever get to feel. One instant headrush – bam! – and a sigh of relief, probably, that I'll never again have to try to be any better than I've so far managed. I can just be truly myself for one moment: ordinary, neither pretty nor ugly, coming up or coming down, and then, as the bright light zaps into ether like a TV screen going blank – not.

22. Animal lover

I was just kicking around, chewing pink bubblegum and letting it burst in a plastic kiss across my face. I was wondering what might be the most modern way to die, right here, right now. The way I imagined it, my bubblegum might splat across my eyes, chemical additives seeping into my retinas and blinding me in several agonizing seconds. Then I might stumble like a once-respectable citizen made suddenly homeless, losing my perspective and self-preserving instincts, smack into a taxi taking office girls to one of their leaving do's. Poignantly, my phone would beep an incoming text message as my mashed up head exhaled its last, bubblegum only partially obscuring my bloodied brains, some of which would be blown in chunks across the nifty shoes of Japanese passers-by. The office girls would bundle out of the taxi, dazed and vaguely miffed that they would have to walk to their trendy bar. I would stain the backseat of the taxi as my cursing, sweating driver swerved around drunken stag and hen parties, lost from Temple Bar, to rush my mortal remains to the Mater, where I would be pronounced DOA. The doctor would absentmindedly hum the theme tune to what was still his favourite TV show, *Friends*, under his breath. One of the junior nurses would remember having seen me in an airport a few years ago, where I would have been practising dance moves and scales to a now very outdated Mariah Carey track, while waiting to collect my luggage from the carousel. My broken bones would be collated, my text message left unread in a mark of respect, as I was stripped to my Calvins, stained blue from my brand new Pash indigo flares, stained brown from my body's expulsion of its last Triple Decker King-Size Meal, and my lithe corpse would be momentarily desired – even in death, it would remain exquisitely toned – before the sickening lust was shoved aside so the last task of plucking glass from my fizz of pubic hair could be performed without violation of my vibrant, dead erection – the last testimony to my lust for life.

I spat my bubblegum into a spiderweb spun between iron railings and made for home, telling myself I was one sick bastard, but a little turned on anyway.

Watching the streets, I realized that life made more sense if you thought of humans as animals – feeding, exchanging, bickering, pissing, grooming, getting on with things, dying, sleeping … what set us apart, except our own sense of importance? But I was boring myself, and it would bore you to go on, and the first rule of the popstar is never to be boring. Keep it catchy!

Moving on.

A man jauntily tipped his cap at me as I passed. I took a moment to recognize him without the usual veil of net curtains. It was like the flipside of seeing your ma in her wedding photo.

'Mr McGinnity! Howaya?'

'Fine and well, son.'

He stopped, so I had to. I put on my friendly face – wider eyes, expectant smile – and thought of what an old-fashioned death Mr McGinnity would have – and soon!

'Anto, son,' – he took my elbow and I involuntarily tensed – 'there's just the one thing I want to say to you.' His hangdog face set gravely.

He paused, framed by the grasping fingers of the dead trees that guard our towerblock. With an effort, I stifled a yawn.

'What?' I said.

'It's this. I know you like your fun –'

I smelled a Christian tirade at this point and turned my friendly face off. But I was wrong.

'Hear me out! I only want to say that fun on street-corners comes with a price. We've got a spare room if you ever need it … urgently.'

Then he tipped his hat further over one lug, winked, grinned, and strolled off like a true Parisian gent. My brain thought *Eh?*, then *Ohhh!*, and I turned to watch his walk, waiting to catch that telltale twitch of the rump that the PC brigade will deny they have – while lisping. Sure enough, it looked to me like Mr McGinnity was genetically programmed to take it up the arse.

Was he for real, or was he a bloody old pervert with spy-holes drilled into the wall of his spare bedroom?

Incidentally, I revised my thoughts on what might be a modern death. Whatever way you look at it, death is both ancient and new – timeless, I suppose – that little black number that never goes out of fashion. I guess that whatever I conjure up as a modern way to die will be superseded by something slicker, or muckier, or maybe just more average than I could imagine now, when the smell of death seems unknowable and sickly glamorous.

23. Playing for the other team

Maybe I would have been good at sport – who knows? As I can dance with flair and precision in line, mime and still look great, I reckon that being a poncey footballer would have been easy. I'm not uncoordinated or out of shape – just look at all the lads who get girlfriends, start drinking and turn lardy at the age of twenty – but all that macho bullshit camaraderie was killer. If you're not part of that team, you can't be a team player.

So when Jenny said that Khalid played football, I thought, *Yep, he must be straight*. I kinda hoped he wasn't, but I thought he had to be. Fags are great at all sorts, but most of us have the decency to leave competitive group sports to the lame-ass heteros who need their man-groping fix to come with a ready-made alibi. 'Honey, the kissing and the hugging and the slapping and the grabbing is a *guy thing*. You just don't get it.'

Then again, I guess that goes for the closet cases too.

This is how it happened. Khalid walked Jenny home after college one day (they were already the gossip of their class) and when a gang of lads chucked a ball at Khalid's head ('Is that cos I'm black?' 'No, it's cos you're ugly!') he waded into the middle of the game, took over the tarmac pitch and scored a hat-trick inside two minutes.

'His dribbling was superb,' Jenny said dreamily.

I made a rude joke – you can make up your own involving 'dribbling' and 'balls' if you like – but the damage was done. Khalid joined the G.A.A. club up beside his flats – the swanks rub shoulders with the knackers these days – and, despite my jealousy and wishful thinking, confirmed his heterosexuality.

I don't have the tits to be a cheerleader, so I decided to become a football fan.

24. The universal dream from nine to five

In the sense that it happens every day, tragedy is normal. Kids get butchered; ma's die of cancer; da's lose themselves to booze and the horses; and I sit here at a computer, mouthing sales-speak inanities into a headset microphone that potentially connects to every brain in this city, in this country – to every eager, waiting, needy brain in the richer half of the world. You probably think that's not very different from being in a boyband, but it's not the kind of exposure I'd hoped for when signing up for megastardom.

I want my face to greet everyone else's in their morning newspaper. I want my voice to be sung along to badly while housewives hoover. I want my smile on bedroom walls where girls sigh and wish I wasn't gay. I want boys to think, *He's hot!* and realize it's OK to think that.

Can we just fast-forward through this work crap? Can we skip it forward a year or so to where I've finished the nine-to-five forever, to where I've survived it as a boring but necessary growing experience on my path to fame and riches?

25. One year later

War goes on and all the papers are still full of it. Fuck that! America almost caused a war between me and my fella last night, when we were down the pub.

He was off on a rant about the two George Bushs, Ronald Reagan, and some dead dudes I've never heard of. He was trying to make a point about how any old retard can achieve status, or something. I don't remember. It came up cos we said so-and-so's boyfriend was retarded. Anyway, me being smart said, 'The president is never who you think it is, he's always just a puppet,' because I was trying to make some point about how retards who achieve status are still retards. I don't remember. But both being stubborn bastards, this became our second row and I almost ended up home alone and dumped.

I chased him, cos he would have been in bits this morning if he didn't get the can of Coke I had in my bag for him – he gets really bad hangovers and it's his last day in work so he doesn't want to take the piss and not show – and, anyway, he relented and came home with me. Decko even saw us on the streetcorner, me putting the can of Coke between us on a litterbin like a truce, and declared it love.

We made love this morning, both of us wanting to make up for the row. (We're such knackers when the beer's in!) We showered and left the house – him late for work and me late with bringing the DVDs back to Chartbusters thanks to our night of kissing and making up, which is cool.

A woman dropped money in the street but I couldn't pick it up because I'd seen who dropped it. I bought our brand-new single, a ballad, which I'm listening to now as the crane I can see from my window breaks up the sky into geometric pieces of sky-blue nothingness.

I also ran into an old flame yesterday. He looked pretty awful, tired and unkempt, but my heart still gave a little jolt. I wondered why we'd gone wrong. Our conversation stuttered, died – or maybe it had been stillborn – and one of those Green Machines that suck up litter came between us. It was time to just *go*.

I threw what was meant to be a light-hearted remark over my shoulder as I left him there, a little bit awkward, a little bit dazed, but he didn't seem to get it – just fluttered his fingertips in goodbye.

I texted him to try and end things on a cheerier note, like the old days.

```
abc              392/1
Grubby! Polish
ur shoes. U could
stick 'em under
the Green
Machine.
     Options
```

But I never got a reply.

Anyway.

Let's go back to where we were.

26. Cathal scores an own goal

'I thought he'd be the only black one,' Cathy said.

'He's the only Brit,' Jenny said.

'Is he any good?' I asked, bewildered by the flurry of limbs and colours on the pitch.

'Yes!' the girls yelled, and I swigged my bottled water and wondered what all the fuss was about.

This is what I saw: arms flapping, cold legs chundering, red faces yelling on the sidelines, guys getting pushed, tugged and tripped, quite a few hungover zombies loitering round the edges, the garish clash of G.A.A. jerseys, short shorts (nice!), mucky turf, a blue sky stuttering cloud like chopped-up lines of coke –

'Keep your eye on the game, Anto!'

Sorry. In short, what I saw was typical straight male awkwardness clunking round a field.

'It's no *Swan Lake.*'

'It's only started.'

'I don't get the rules.'

'But you played football in school for years!'

'I didn't *play* it, I was just *there.*'

'Didn't you pick it up?'

'It's incomprehensible. Like, what are all the little flags for?'

'There aren't any little flags.'

'Oh. Yeah.'

'Just watch Khalid,' Jenny said. 'He's deadly.'

So I just watched Khalid.

I had to admit, there was something more … graceful about him. He was slimmer than most of our chunkified Irish chaps. He didn't scramble as madly as they did. He seemed to be watching the game as well as insinuating himself through it –

'GOAL!'

'Huh? How did that happen? Who scored?'

'Khalid did, you fucking eejit!'

'But I only saw him jump!'

'It was a header, you spa!'

I joined in the yelling – 'Nice legs, Kashani!' – and got told to shut up by my giggly girlfriends. Don't you just love your straight mates? They're so shockable.

'Gotta use the jacks.'

'Ooh, be careful.'

I jogged off for a quick piss as Khalid was engulfed in a congratulatory orgy.

The toilets were concrete, like something out of communism. There were no mirrors! Someone had blown chunks in one of the urinals but, as always, I made a detour to a cubicle, being the performance-anxiety type when it comes to public peeing. Fag!

I heard someone lurch in after me to gush like a racehorse against the wall. I flushed and tried to look butch as I strode out of the cubicle, very much *not* glancing towards the urinals, when a voice called me back.

'Anto!'

'Eh? Oh, hi. Howaya?'

Cathal made a big deal about waggling his cock about. He took ages stuffing it back in his tracksuit bottoms as he rolled over, round-shouldered and high-coloured, talking about something – I can't remember what – and looking me straight in the eye in a way he never did. I was deaf and dumb. I was thinking about how much I used to fancy him at school, and how he'd gradually turned into this slightly bloated, slightly stupid version of himself, drunk and just out of reach. I suppose that's not unusual. It's how we all turn into the generation gone before, replicating our parents' weaknesses, never managing to be quite good enough, earn enough, love enough, care enough, stay well long enough to try and right all the wrongs we choose to do, or fall into despite our ideals. I saw Cathal's ordinary life unfurl in his drink-glazed eyes and slow, wet lips mouthing all those things he would regret when he sobered up.

'Funny to see you here!'

'Yeah.'

'I love your da. He's the man … We should, y'know … We should …'

Was I imagining his eyes sliding towards the cubicle?

'Remember how we used to …? I miss the way we used to …'

His hand slipped to his crotch.

'Hang …'

He couldn't be …?

'Eh, we better get back to the match.'

'Yeah, yeah. Defo. Good match. Some talent, huh?'

'Yeah!'

We grinned, I think, conspiratorially. I had to lead Cathal out the door, his body falling into mine, lighter than I would have imagined, his lips at my neck, murmuring.

'I really, really hope to see you after the match.'

'Sure.'

'No. Really. I really, really hope so.'

'OK.'

'Do you understand?'

Suddenly serious, he held me by the shoulders, here, in the open air, as the teams played on, my da shouting on the sideline, and the fans, the lads, the girlfriends and ma's and sisters and toddlers all wailed and stomped and laughed and yawned and then he kissed me.

He did. He kissed me on the neck, with one hand at my waist and another in my hair. I kissed him back, softly, in his ear, not knowing quite what I was doing, and then I was walking in the sunlight – a crisper, cleaner day than I remembered – shocked, excited, disbelieving what we'd done.

I didn't watch the rest of the match. I sat there rehearsing how to approach Cathal again – did he really want to see me? in public? – as my da's team and Khalid's team fought it out. I didn't spot Khalid's hat-trick, or the foul that landed Ken flat on his arse and then on a stretcher, or my da's rage as his team were swiftly annihilated.

I followed Cathal's path around the pitch, muzzy as a bumblebee. When the final score was announced he fell backwards, laughing, drunk, a bottle of Bud fallen from his fist, an embarrassment to the team he'd been too 'unwell' to play for today. I left him lying there to be picked up by someone else and followed the girls into town, where Jenny was meeting Khalid.

The bar we went to was like any other uber-streamlined/blond-wooded/aluminium-cooled/lighting-concealed/strategically-mirrored/leather-couched/suede-cubed/invisibly-waitroned lounges I feel so comforted by. Vast anonymous canvases soothed our brows. The music was barely there.

'Why are all the best places gay?' Khalid said.

'This place isn't gay.'

'It looks gay,' Jenny and Clare said in unison.

'Oh, you people. You think everywhere *blank* has to be gay because it's *tasteful* and it's *empty*. All this,' I spread my arms wide, '*nothingness* makes you think of *death* and you think that just cos we don't *breed* we never *live*.' I sipped my gin and slim, quite exhausted.

'There are lots of lesbian mothers nowadays,' Cathy said, a bit upset.

'I just thought that waiter was too cute,' Jenny muttered.

'You can raise one of my kids, Anto,' Khalid said. Jenny looked at him sharply and I beamed right back at our new local god.

'You know what, Anto?' Khalid continued. 'We should hang out. I need more cool friends.'

What can I say? Flattery works.

27. The things they did and didn't do

Round her flat, they did the dishes together. He took her on a horse-and-cart trip around Stephen's Green, which was a very British touristy thing to do, I thought. Jenny is allergic to horses and came home afterwards to get her anti-histamines, her face puffed up like popcorn.

'He kissed me with me eyes streamin'!'

He sent her presents in the post, silly things like a badge that said, 'I AM 4!' or a novelty photo-booth photo of him as a cowboy, or a Cadbury's Creme Egg (which I devoured, my fingernails painted in her vermilion varnish).

'I'm glad you ate it, I hate them! They're rotten. But I wouldn't want to hurt his feelings ...'

They studied most days in the library together – *quelle* bore. I met them a couple of times in Trinity for lunch. They were famous in the Arts Block – it doesn't take much.

Jenny insisted they weren't shagging, which I took as an encouraging sign.

She even invited him to dinner one evening. Zak thought that would be cool – 'He's a geezer!' – and Ma was secretly flustered. 'But Anto,' she asked me on the sly, 'what do they eat?'

Da was a total cunt. 'That poncey yoke who scored the hat-trick?' he scoffed. 'He's black, he's a Brit, and he looks every inch the bum-boy!' Da glared at me as if that was my fault.

I was delighted.

28. Love

Most people define their lives according to their loves. When I look back at different times in my life, I don't think about the crappy job I had then, or what music I was into – I think about whomever I found myself in love with. The chap I was seeing, or the one I couldn't have, the guy who liked me but I couldn't like him back.

Like anyone, I can't tell you what love means. You find your own definition, I suppose.

'When I found myself ironing his underpants, I knew it was love.'

'I only realized I loved that girl on her wedding day. I slit my wrists beneath the dinner table while her husband made the speech. I was hospitalized and they flew off to Biarritz.'

'The way he listens to me talk about the dreams I dreamt last night. No one really finds that interesting. It must be love ...'

It's the most powerful thing, to be a part of someone else's history. I still find it hard to come to terms with the idea of being a part of another person's story. It must be the megalomaniac in me. When I'm comfortable with that, with being just a player in the story of my life, with my life story being inextricably strung together with one other person's, I think I'll have found true love.

29. The sky reflects a concrete grey

I woke up in a strop, the temporary depression of a desperate, failing wannabe.

I leapt out of bed, forgetting it was my day off. It only dawned on me as I soaped myself, scalded under the shower – Zak and Ma raising a ruckus at the door, cos they were running late and I was just standing there, naked and dazed and with suds in my eyes – *I was nobody*.

It came as a shock. Here I was, just a chap, another naked no one, with a day off work and no immediate channel for his creative urges. It was so depressing I couldn't even work up the enthusiasm for a wank, and I stumbled – fluffy round the edges – from the bathroom, mopey as a little kicked puppy dog.

Zak sang at the top of his voice, which is always a pain in the ass, cos he's better than me. Ma was trailing some monologue around every room, her words vapourizing at my unheeding ears, as I sat on Zak's bottom bunk, staring at my mess of smelly socks and pants. Zak has always been scrupulously tidy – I'm the one who leaves the place like a tip, as if our room is my personal walk-in wardrobe. *Christ*, I thought, *he sings better. He's tidy. He'd make an even better gayer than I do.*

'Will you do that for me?' Ma said, popping her head around the door.

'What?'

'Do you ever listen to a word I say?'

I threw a rolled-up sock at her, but she swatted it back at me with her sociology textbook. It thwacked me on the nose.

'Ring your sister!'

'Which one?'

'Jennifer!' she yelled, walloping off to college.

Zak did a little dance around the bedroom as he got dressed for school, singing some Latino pop song that I hadn't learned the moves for yet. I lobbed a couple of socks at him and he headed them back at me.

'My evil sock attack has backfired. Twice.'

'Ah, go back to bed.'

'Can't. Up. Awake. Wah!'

'You'll be famous one day, bro,' Zak said. 'Chill!'

I couldn't though. I watched some breakfast TV, drank a week's worth of coffee (our manager should count herself lucky that ODing on caffeine is my one occupational hazard), borrowed Zak's runners and went for a traipse around wherever my new fat feet would take me.

I had my headphones on – Danni Minogue, cos she's the underdog – and felt invisible, locked in my own little world. The world outside was just fleeting impressions – strangers' glances, blank, oblivious or blatant; dog shit; changing traffic lights; signs in shop windows. Cars crawled, as if they had a choice. Pigeons nubbled along the pavements, greedy and stupid and really kind of ugly now I noticed. All belly and no brain. Their eyes were just dots, big enough only to see the food in front of them. Their feet looked like rubber. It seemed obscene that something capable of flight could choose to spend its time squabbling in gutters.

Why wasn't I famous yet?

I sat by the river. The rushes were so tall and elegant they looked fake, impossible. The grasses were shaggy, like giant eighties perms, like Tina Turner had dumped her old wigs off the side of the bridge. Conga lines of little ducks swept by on the current. I watched an early morning jogger pass a clump of winos. Lucky bastards. *They* didn't have to worry about clawing their way to superstardom.

The lull of the river soothed me a little. I made my way home with a cleaner brain, the static erased by the spool-like tape of brown water.

Most mornings, the unforgiving clarity of sunlight inspires me to mentally colour the grime of our towerblock with imaginary rainbows. Today, I decided that if I couldn't tear the place down brick by brick, I could at least spring-clean our flat.

I hoovered, swept, did the breakfast dishes, sponged the skirting boards, scrubbed the hob, dusted, threw out heaps of old magazines, tidied my bedroom, emptied ashtrays and washed them out, went mad with bleach in the toilet and bathroom.

I'm going to end up a nudie houseboy.

After a couple of hours spic-and-spanning, I flopped on the couch, stuck on the telly and rang Jenny.

'Hey Anto, what's up?'

'Howaya Jen, nothing, Ma just said to give you a buzz.'

'Why?'

'I dunno, she just said. Were you talking to her?'

'Oh Anto,' Jenny sighed. 'I broke up with Khalid.'

Yes!

'Oh Jen, that's awful ...'

Heh heh heh!

I listened, consoled, agreed it was all for the best, secretly plotting my next move.

Drink, I think.

Through the window, I saw a suitcase spilling clothes tumble from the floor above. The thuds of bashing feet and fists shook the ceiling. Our home gleamed amid the concrete grey, for now, for a little while.

30. Drinking in the flowers

We went knacker-drinking in Stephen's Green. The flowers clashed all around us, the fountain spritzed tourists' fingers, the lazy sprawls of back-packers chorused a jabbering soundtrack to our little depression session.

'Will you miss Jenny?'

'Yeah, I will miss her. Though I see her every day.'

'That's worse.'

'Nah, it's OK.'

The sun was baking us like gingerbread men stretched out on a big green baking tray. I could feel the freckles popping into life across my nose. I wondered if Khalid tanned easily but was afraid to ask in case it was racist.

'Let's not talk about her. Let's talk about you, man. Have you had many boyfriends?'

'Um, a few. Nothing very serious.'

'Go on, tell me about them. Who was your first?'

'Oh god – I was only twelve! Does that count?'

'Twelve? Was he your priest?'

'Fuck off! I'm not into men in dresses. He was this guy at school, we played football together and used to mess around afterwards. I thought we'd get married!'

'Did you last long?'

'I dunno, maybe … eight months? Oh, it's so embarrassing, you know Confirmation?'

'Yeah.'

'Well you know the way you have to choose a name? I chose his!'

'What's your Confirmation name?'

'Bernard.'

'Ugh!' Khalid laughed. 'It must have been love!'

'He got married last year, got some girl pregnant. He asked me to the wedding and everything.'

'Is he bisexual?'

'Nah, he's straight.'

'Even though ...? Did you put him off men?'

'Probably. My cock was too big for his poor little bum.'

'Really?'

'Yeah.'

'Wow,' Khalid said, eyes twinkling like fairy lights. 'And you're not even black.'

'Oh, shut up,' I said, secretly loving it. 'It was painful for me too, you know. I had a really sore cock and I had to go to the doctor's, I didn't know *what* was wrong, but I told my ma my mickey was killing me and she *dragged* me to the doctor, who was a *woman.*'

'Ouch.'

'So the woman doctor zipped me open and, eh, examined me, and actually *winked* at my ma. "Growing pains," she said. "He'll be grateful in a few years."'

'I'll have to get a peek, see if you're as big as the black man.'

'Cheeky bugger.'

'We're rude, we are. So what other boyfriends have you had?'

I told him about Anto (issues), Mark (baggage), Rock (we're still mates), Alex (fat), Dave (geek), David (don't ask), Paul (moved to London), and the latest, Kieran (psycho).

'Everyone,' I said, 'has at least one psychotic ex-boyfriend. Hardly surprising, I mean, homophobia isn't good for your health. But he started spray-painting his bedroom walls with verses from the Bible, so he had to go.'

'Jenny's a bit religious, isn't she?'

'Yeah, well, I'm not. Though some of those Scientologists who catch you unawares on the street are really cute. I think they do it on purpose.'

'*He's* cute,' Khalid said, nodding at a bare-limbed boy swishing past. 'Do you like him?'

'Do *you* like him?'

Khalid laughed and poured some cider down his neck. 'I'm straight. But I'm ... *intrigued* by the gay scene. You'll have to take me out – we can find you a boyfriend!'

'Well, thanks,' I murmured.

Khalid raised a toast – 'To the gay life!' – and when he smiled at me, the flowers surrounding us ceased to clash, fine-tuning their colours like the sudden harmony of a glorious pop song.

31. Monkey meets junkie

So I started hanging out with Khalid, just for something to do in-between unpromising band rehearsals and putting my personality on hold for work. He was kind of quiet, which meant I could show off. He was fascinated with gay stuff ('Do you know many bisexuals?' 'Do you like sucking cock?' 'There aren't many black gay guys, are there?') and I thought he was confused, but sweet. Sometimes, when he leant in too close, I thought he might be trying something on – but I didn't want to be anyone's experimental sexual springboard. I'd had enough of that, as I kept reminding myself, trying not to notice his slyly kissable lips, his easily distracted, slightly out-of-focus eyes, his tousled hair … *yeah, yeah, yeah.*

We shopped together. I tried to stop him buying patterned boxers and he helped me choose some girly tops for going out. He even shaved my back so I could wear them without looking too much like a monkey in drag. One night I was skipping home after a quiet pint together ('Talking to you is like talking to Jennifer') when some junkie I didn't even recognize started following me home.

'Have you –'

'No.'

'You dunno –'

'No, sorry.'

'I like your hair!' he shouted after me, as I turned by the nightly pool of orange crush spilled by the streetlight on our corner.

'Thanks!' I said, swivelling to dazzle my heroin-scuzz friend with an All-American smile.

He hung in a shadow like a bug in a web, arms jerking as he conjured imaginary styles from his fingertips. 'But you should have, you know, a big red stripe down the middle, that'd be deadly!'

He kept on shouting after me. My home, a dark box of air suspended in the sky by the toxic dreams of a city, loomed.

It wasn't fabulous, stumbling into the belly of our block of flats while heroin addicts dispensed fashion advice from the street beyond. The steps smelled ripe – I felt I could smell them with my skin – and would continue to do so, with or without my alcoholic breath to feed them.

I almost threw up, swallowed it, and thought, *I need a new life.*

32. Planning for the future

Have you ever tried to flat-hunt in Dublin? Don't. Book yourself into a nice kennel instead. Boxes of rot are being flogged as habitable living spaces. The dominant colour scheme is the ground-in brown of Homeless Person's Face. The furniture has been purchased with Esso tokens from the out-of-town warehouses of late-eighties stockpiled reject specimens. And the Legoland apartments! Rock memorably described them as 'ice-cream parlours with no ice cream'. I admire their blank, cool glare, but I'm not sure we can afford to rent one and still eat. Decko and I made a pact that if we ever get porky, we're signing up straight away.

Decko and I wanted a place together, two rooms being essential. Can you imagine two prima donnas fighting over the same mirror? To distract ourselves from the weekly trundle round overpriced hovels on our respective days off, we'd each of us, in turn, take our skinny ass to the Front Lounge for an afternoon latte (the gayest of coffees) and, in my case, an outside smoke. I'd watch carcinogenic whispers sublimate between my mouth and the sky, trying to envisage my perfect life.

How would I cope with constant touring, strings of hotels, the paparazzi, the free drugs, the firing of managers and the hiring of stylists, the image changes, the number ones, the endless bloody *promotion*, the early morning kids' TV? How would I cope when it was over too soon, when I had only my wealth and the odd where-are-they-now column to add to my personal scrapbook collection? How could I cope with being me again?

I couldn't imagine it. I couldn't imagine existing in a timeless capsule of youth and being envied. I couldn't imagine anything other than this, other than striving for it, and I worried that that meant I was only destined for *wanting*. I bet Madonna never had doubts.

Meanwhile, I drank my coffee alone, smoked, and thought of Khalid. It's not my fault. Aren't the working classes conditioned to see life as an impossible struggle? To pretend to themselves that things will all work out for the best? Meaning that someone else can foot the bill for your coffin when you die alone and penniless in a gutter.

What I needed was a plan. I bet Madonna made plans …

33. Options

abc   444/1
U awake Khalid?
    Options

YEP
    Options

abc   449/1
What doin?
    Options

WATCHING THE
BOX. WISH WE
HAD A TV
    Options

abc   360/1
I have a TV.
Well, a
transvestite.
Once u plug her
in, she's turned
on all nite. How
was the party?
    Options

IT WAS ALMOST
AS GOOD AS LIFE
ITSELF. I
EMBRACED ALL
THE
COCKSANDTITS.
ALMOST GOT
BRICKED ON WAY
HOME. IT WAS A
COWARDLY
GESTURE. I HATE

COWARDS – WHAT
DO U HATE?
   Options

abc   362/1
I hate work, &
bars that close
early – drives
me beserk &
memories of
child psychiatry
anger me.
   Options

CHILD
PSYCHIATRY –
INTERESTING.
MOST PEOPLE
WOULD HAVE SAID
CHILD
PORNOGRAPHY
   Options

abc   312/1
Yeah that 2 ya
morbid
bedwetter. Tell
u what, I'm tired
of bein out of
love. I hate that
2. Want 2 fall all
over again.
Break my heart.
Or my arse.
   Options

I MAY WET THE
BED BUT BELIEVE
ME – I HAVE FUN
DOING IT. BREAK
YOUR
ARSE/HEART – DO
U MEAN
PHYSICALLY ?
   Options

66

abc   361/1
Of course
break=
physically
nothing else
exists. Or at
least, it's more
fun 2 believe
that. Yeah!
     Options

I'M TOUCHED
THAT I AM IN A
POSITION 2
BREAK YOUR
HEART. I FEEL
DANGEROUS WITH
THIS
POWER...SMOKIN
G.BE SURE NOT
TO PISS ME OFF
     Options

abc   337/1
Hey Mr Ego – did
I say u could
break my heart?
U ain't
dangerous & I is
2 sexy 4 ya, ya
eejit boy. But we
all beautiful.
     Options

2 SEXY 4 ME ?
WHEN WAS THE
LAST TIME I
EJACULATED IN
YOUR SMALL
PRESENCE?
     Options

abc   248/2
Hmmm, prob' ly
when u shaved
my back so I cd

wear that
see-thru vest. &
I thought that
was shaving
foam! & if u must
know, I ain't
small where it
counts. OK, enuff
about my fab
self. Tell me
sumfink about
urself
    Options

TALKING ABOUT
SEX DEPRESSES
ME
    Options

abc   304/1
Let's talk about
food. I like
chocolate,
coffee, & sushi
(cos it's modern,
decadent &
cute). & dirty
burgers on the
way home from
drunken lunacy
(knacker!)
    Options

I LIKE FULL
ENGLISH
BREAKFASTS AND
THE SKIN OF AN
IRISH CHICKEN
    Options

abc   332/1
U have good
taste. I'm
starving now.
Bad rain on the
windows. Bad

company outside
windows. Am
planning life
after
Christchurch.
   Options

U NEED TASTY
FOOD TO MAKE
UP 4
CUNNILINGUS.
ANYWAY HOW'S
THE HOUSE
SEARCH? WHERE
DO BROKEN
HEARTS GO?
   Options

abc   319/1
The
search=crap.
Stuck at home.
Broken hearts
go 2 the George,
get pissed,
dance like a
bastard & snog
random
strangers. Is ur
heart broken?
   Options

I'M SURVIVING.
FIRST TIME IT'S
BEEN BROKEN.
SHOULD
RECOVER
   Options

abc   434/1
Anything I can
do 2 help?
   Options

**DO U HAVE
ANOTHER
SISTER?**
  Options

abc   385/1
Eh, yeah. But
she's spoken 4.
The 2 chaps r
free tho. Mind
u, Zak's only 15.
  Options

**YOU SEEM TO BE
THE BEST OF A
GOOD BUNCH.
DADDY MUST
HAVE MAGIC
BEANS**
  Options

abc   14
Here, u can have
mine. I don't
need it anyway.
  Options

**I AIN'T GETTING
WHAT YOU'RE
TRYING 2 SEND,
I'M CONSIDERING
GOING 2 BED AS I
NEED 2 GET UP
EARLY 2 GO 2
GALWAY. SO IF U
NEED 2 SAY
SOMETHING,
NOW'S THE TIME.**
  Options

abc   310/1
Nah, I just tried
2 send u a
picture msg of a
heart & msg
saying u can
have mine. It's
been used,
bruised, abused
& confused but
hey, u need it
more than I do.
    Options

THAT WAS SUCH A
SWEET MESSAGE!
U DESERVE
SOMEONE GOOD.
& SOMEWHERE 2
LIVE
    Options

abc   397/1
Yeah. Just don't
tell anyone how
lovely I am. Nite
nite Khalid.
    Options

GOODNIGHT
ANTO
    Options

34. Seconds of light

'Sweetie!' Terry said. 'One word! *Muslim*.'

A girl selling pretzels from a basket floated past. We murmured, 'No, thanks,' and sipped our pints. No one wanted to touch The Religious Issue.

'Well,' I said. 'He drinks, and Muslims aren't supposed to drink. He was going out with Jenny, and she's Catholic ...'

'Sweetie, I'm not even *touching* that one. Trying to jump your sister's ex? That's *déclassé*.'

'At least it's true to form,' Decko said. 'He's straight. Apparently.'

'Do it,' Rock said. 'Just get him drunk and hop on him. If he's got a penis, he won't say no.'

'Speaking of which, have you seen it yet?' Brendan asked.

'No. Though he wants to see mine.'

'Ah!'

'Well there you go,' Rock decided. 'Lads get drunk, oh, show me yours and I'll show you mine, nature takes its course. You've got nothing to lose,' he concluded, 'but a good friend, your dignity and your self-respect. And maybe your sister.'

'Can't it be more romantic than that?' I wondered, gloomily.

'No,' everyone chorused.

'I think it's a bit late for romance,' Brendan said. 'It's a nice idea, but at this stage, getting drunk together is the only option. I wouldn't be surprised if he never spoke to you again afterwards, though.'

'At least you'd have closure,' Rock said.

The evening light pixellated through the tall glass windows like a computer screen glitching before a virus kicks in. A young guy, whom I knew as an actor, let his thin fingers play the piano as his pretty voice threaded a tune through the silver-white notes. The music spun and spiralled through the bar, nestling in our hair like ribbons of lace, connecting us all, drinkers, talkers, listeners, loners, in a network of noise we barely noticed.

35. A design for life

Jenny's mantra for life is, 'Me man, me tan, me style, me flat and me first!' With her year-round tan and her crushing style – boots, fur collars, retro prints – she has no trouble finding interested men. They're usually knackers though ('like *ourselves*, of course') which is more amusing but not fabulous.

Her flat was always immaculate, her allergies flatlined in the formidable cleanliness and efficient beauty of her all-girl household. She encouraged one of her mousy-brown flatmates to go golden blonde, the other to go red, and she dyed her own dark locks deep black to complete the seventies theme of their home. Despite claiming failure every time, she always pulled Firsts in her exams. Jennifer believes in positivity, and good things happen to her.

Her men though! It wasn't long before she was dating another camp chap, Aaron. He was quite posh. He dressed like one of the *Dawson's Creek* boys and bought Ma chocolates. You could tell he'd never been in an inner-city flat before, but Jenny insisted he come around to see it for himself. He was very polite.

'We're not as swanky as him, you know,' she confided. 'The toilet in his house makes no noise when you flush it and his ma only ever buys white towels. Can you imagine?'

I could, and I was jealous.

36. Almost summer

I was listless, spending hours posing in front of the mirror, smoking endless cigarettes. The mirror smoked back at me, holding my gaze, holding me immobile as smoke seduced my fingertips, teasing, and vanished. I stubbed the butts out in the sink, played with my hair, pouted. I ran my hands over the stubble on my shoulders and back, considering the growth since Khalid had swept his hands along my skin. I tried to catch a pose that might make someone fall in love.

I ran baths, ignored the bangings on the door, smoked some more, pitched the butts into the toilet bowl. As my extremities wrinkled, I thought about nothing. I would let the water run out and feel it sucking at my skin. I would lie for a while, cooling corpse-like while the blood sank to my legs. I would shiver myself dry and flush the toilet of the cigarette filters that floated like dead squashed goldfish in the lightly bleached water.

Outside, the evenings hung around lazily. They fuzzed around the edges, blushing into the night. The world as I see it is populated with idiots and punctuated by violence. I would like to blend with the idiots, to become idiotic too, to be happily doped up on TV and the false comfort of belief. I usually fall for ordinary guys, the sort that don't like to think too much. They're often beautiful – I remember Karl's tip-tilted nose, Enda's cat-like eyes, Billy's cute sticky-out ears – and maybe kind of dumb. Not stupid. Just unaware of their beauty, unsure of their place in the world. Ultimately, losers. Never grasping their own potential enough to really make it. Khalid's beauty lies in his soft skin and biteable lips. I wanted to save him, and I couldn't, of course.

I wanted to stand him in the middle of his room and strip him slowly. I wanted to puzzle over every part of exposed flesh and absorb it piece by piece, through my eyes and through my touch. I wanted to shove my head between his legs, put my tongue in his ass and feel him tremble. I wanted him to wonder why I liked looking at him so much. I wanted to feel him come alive inside his skin.

I wanted to shout at him, 'Don't you know what this world's like?

Don't you know that everything in it, everything, is product? Don't you know that everything we feel, everything we think we want is made up of tiny little components of corporate endorsement? Don't you know you're beautiful, you're special to me, you'll cease to exist, I'm the only chance you've got?'

I love guys who know life is difficult, who know that nothing matters, who still listen to cheerful crappy pop.

37. Trinity Ball champagne

We tripped over the heroin kids on our way in the door. The chocolate wrappers they'd used to cook up were lying around, the chocolate crushed into the steps of the apartment block.

The girls weren't nearly ready, lashing on the mascara, twirling under perfumes, trying on their every pair of shoes. 'The cobblestones? To hell with them – I'm wearing my highest heels!'

The lads had beer and the girls had vodka. Aaron even brought champagne. I wasn't really drinking because I wasn't going with them, I was only there to photograph the glamour.

'Anto, zip me up!'

'Anto, do my back!'

I could have felt like Cinderella, except it was fun. The worst bit was watching the brick-faced dentist flirting with the American exchange girl. He had all the finesse of a slab of ham. Jenny tried to get Aaron to dance, but he was stoically stuck into the drink. His mate was down from Belfast; the plan was to get Greta to snog him. She would – she was hammered.

I spent a while on the balcony, watching the torches from Smithfield bleach the city rooftops. The light lay on buildings like the memory of snow.

Couples yelled in the streets, scrapping under billboards, re-enacting scenes from *Ricki Lake*. Aaron and his mate – I don't remember if I ever knew his name – joined me outside. We spat across the cars, revenge for the wailing alarms that didn't alarm anyone, just put them off their TV till they filtered it from their consciousness. We soon didn't notice it.

The talk turned to the summer, what we were all going to do. Probably something like getting drunk in afternoons, sunburning, half falling in love with every other face we would catch a glimpse of gliding by on buses … yeah.

'Hey guys! Greta is doing "Private Dancer"!'

Greta giggled and wriggled for us one by one, as Tina Turner aurally raped us. With her hands on my hips, I tucked Suzie's Limited Edition Marvel Comic Monopoly Money in Greta's shimmering cleavage, before tossing the rest to the ceiling.

Thousands of theoretical dollars died in mid-air, fluttering down upon us like the shed wings of butterflies, crisp, soulless, as if summer were already over.

The camera flashed off the splinters in the heart of the ice in the vodka, facial glitter, the silver orchid in the American student's hair, new cufflinks, teeth. Greta popped the champagne as a finale. I drank mine from a mug.

'It's only cheap stuff,' Aaron apologized, but that was fine. The cheap champagne smelled like Khalid's skin. I rolled it on my tongue. It vanished.

It somehow took us half an hour more to leave. Jenny lost Aaron on the way to her taxi. She thought he'd left her. His mate and I helped Greta downstairs – the lift was broken – and they were in each other's arms by the second floor. The others slid between couples in threes and fours. Two, I think, of Suzie's exes were there, so she had to avoid an awkward pairing up.

I found Aaron waiting for Jenny round the corner of the apartment block. He was staring at his feet.

I gave it two weeks.

38. When networks fall

'Naomi's skirt got ripped and her phone was stolen by some posh knacker. We were hammered and we lost each other inside for, like, half an hour. The bands were shite, well, no one goes for the music but I thought the Abba tribute band was a laugh. Mairéad declared her undying love for Vince, but he said to Will that he'd thought *they* were practically boyfriends all of last year. She's obsessed with him and he's obsessed with Will. He'll deny it when he sobers up. Elaine didn't get in and I heard from Fiona that she had a huge row with the bouncers so *of course* she didn't get in, she's a *mess* when she's drunk. I kept running into Gervaise.'

Jennifer swirled the last of the Paracetemol round in her glass before tipping it down her throat.

'There were all sorts riding on the cricket pitch but most people just passed out. Oh yeah, there was dodgy E going round and Fearghal sent Alistair's flatmate's friend's friend out of his room. Fearghal was doing room checks and this guy was hiding in the wardrobe trying to get in for free, they were raging! Tried to bribe him with a bottle of vodka. Someone puked in Thomas's shoes. He took them off to dance. I was wrecked so I zonked out for a bit in the Buttery, it was hell, so loud and dark and like the only thing you could eat were those minging burgers. Yeah. They had burger stalls in Front Arch. I swear, you should get a good feed for the money you're paying. Insurance me arse. Who's insured? My heels weren't insured, I'll tell you that, me feet are killin' me. Oh yeah, someone pushed someone over in a Portaloo. He must've been covered in shite! The lads all were just pissing up against House Six. Will won the Fancy Dress, no, the Best Dressed Guy? Was that it? Yeah. He was in tops and tails and a ruffled shirt. Some model won the girls' bit, she was in the ad so it was all a scam, fair play to her, I would've scammed it too! She was *stunning*. I was bloody *starving* all night and *sooo* drunk. I hardly saw anyone I knew, I never realized there were so many bodies at Trinity. They're all wankers. There were quite a few gayers, you should go next year. This Malaysian guy was in drag, I said, "Ooh, you look cool," he said it was his ma's traditional dress! That was cool. I have a million photos but everyone looks awful, probably. Pissed. There were girls bawling everywhere and the amount of lost people ... Ed got a quote in the *Indo*, we think, must buy it. Oh God, I'm going to puke –'

I waited until Jennifer came scurrying back from the toilet before popping the *real* question.

'Yeah, I saw Khalid, yeah, he had some girl on his arm but he kept flirting and asking Aaron if he was gay. Sad bastard. Did you see what Sabrina was wearing? Her man bought everyone drinks and met some fella he knew from years ago, mad. He's from Monaghan, is that in the North? I dunno either. I wonder what happened to Pamela? The network went down at about two in the morning, couldn't text or ring anyone, nightmare. Good job I found Lorraine, oh my God, she had the night from hell – '

I'd heard all I needed to.

Khalid had a *woman*.

39. Obsessive compulsive love disorder

People swarmed around me. I found myself standing still, quite suddenly, at any moment. I might be buying ice cream or glancing at new model MP3 players in a glossy shop window. I could be eating chips or forgetting where I'd thrown my black V-neck lycra T-shirt. Sometimes it would hit me mid-sentence and acquaintances started to stare at me strangely, fazed by my random instant meltdown. Had someone pulled a plug? Was I glitching? Would a tentative smile reboot my system?

I was in love. Or at least *obsessed*.

I was surprised they didn't see tiny little Khalids dancing in my pupils. To others, a virus, but to me, a drug; the physical elation at the thought of his presence, the surrender when he arrived, smelling like himself, utterly alive in a way that made me feel drawn and two-dimensional.

I wanted to dedicate my songs to his smile, to the way he pulled at his earlobe when distracted, to the louche slink of his walk along the high street – yeah, like that had never been done before. All we seemed to do was browse, and drink, and find new ways to tease each other's curiosity – with the latest cocktail, b-side remixes, for-no-reason idiotic text messages.

> **IS CRAIG DAVID**
> **GAY ?**
> **Options**

> abc   399/1
> **How wd I know?**
> **I heard a vicious**
> **rumour that he's**
> **black tho.**
> **Options**

Later, when it was over, when the comedowns started to outweigh the highs, I began to wonder if the good times had been real. When you fall out with a mate, does it negate the good times you had? Can you remember moments and smile for what they alone contained, without the shadow of hindsight whispering 'Delusion!' in your ear?

DESPITE YOUR
SEX APPEAL – I'M
STILL STRAIGHT !
Options

Like good pop music, love is generic. It slips into your life as if it has always existed, waiting to be discovered, and when you fall for it, you wonder how you ever coped without its shiny promise. This does not make it any less real, though those who've never known the joys of either love or pop will always deny their validity or cynically attempt to sell their manufactured equivalent to people who can't tell the difference, who will consume greedily, endlessly, and ultimately emptily. For those who recognize the real thing, it doesn't matter how many others feel the same, you experience the thrill uniquely. It doesn't matter that our pure, pleasure-seeking chemical reactions are mass-produced if our hormones sing in harmony to the world we create around us.

40. Persuasion

Rock was back from Munich, though it could have been anywhere, really. I met him in town for some coffee and overpriced cake. He ordered a Danish – 'The Amish dessert,' he muttered, as the waitron plonked a mouldy spiral of poo in front of him. Mine was a much more fabulous fusion – bannoffee – and was presented in a Jackson Pollock of chocolate sauce.

'Wow! That's such a gay dessert!'

'Thank you. Now tell me all about Munich.'

Rock had been whisked off to Germany by his wealthy Malaysian boyfriend, who had to remain closeted in case his family disinherited him of their vast fortune. Rock and Kevin (of all the Western names to choose!) favoured holidays involving sightseeing (you can take the queen out of Malaysia ...) and scouring the local saunas for rough trade.

'We had our first threesome!'

'Huh?'

'Our first together, I mean. Oh, and I hit an all-new record of sleaze!' Rock declared with glee, licking crumbs from his deft little fingers.

'Scare me.'

'It was with ... *a rent boy!*'

'OK. So it was like when we were together, except – you did it?'

When Rock and I were going out, this guy chatted me up, but I said no, cos of Rock. He was lovely, like Stephen Gately's cheeky little brother. He said my having a boyfriend wasn't a problem, and bought us both a drink (I insisted on doubles). Anyway, it turned ugly when I turned him down for a threesome – 'But we've all kissed! I bought you a drink! You have to!' – and Rock and I left pretty sharpish. When I ran into him a couple of weeks later, I insisted on buying him a drink back, and he insisted on pulling out a wad of notes to show he didn't need me to pay for anything. 'Jesus!' I said. 'What are you? A drug dealer or a rent boy?' but he just laughed, drank his whiskey and shook my hand. I've only seen him once since, touting for business down by the Liffey.

'Haha, sort of!' Rock said. 'Except Kevin sorted it all out. He was straight, apparently, so he didn't kiss. He had no problem rimming and sucking my cock though!'

'How much?'

'Eighty.'

'I hope Kevin paid!'

'Halfsies. Oh well, I was pissed and it didn't last too long.'

'A new low,' I said, resigned.

The truth is, Rock wouldn't need to go to saunas if he'd just cut his hair. It's a bleach-blond bob that makes him look like a leftover lesbian from 1982. I made a mental note to fashion him a little beginner's guide to haircuts.

'I mean, two years on, boyfriends get boring,' Rock said.

'Kevin was always boring. Maybe you need a new boyfriend.'

'But he brings me on holidays! Ooh, the rent boy was such a cutie, and he talked about his girlfriend ...'

And so I decided to seduce Khalid, before I found myself paying some rent boy to wear his stolen underwear and call me Jennifer.

While sorting out the bill, Rock told me his dad had been diagnosed with cancer: 'Let's face it though, we're all going to get it. Where do you expect yours?' He went to visit him in hospital, and I made for home.

On the way, three drunken lads were rolling round an alleyway, shouting about their lack of future: 'You, me, him, none of us are going anywhere! You're as much stuck here as – quit moaning! What have you got to moan about, more than any of us?'

Someone pushed someone into a car. I hung back, not wanting to get into a row. The light from the street lamp streaked across my sunglasses in rotating bands, like computerized flowers. I watched a plane, or rather, a glowing red dot, trail against the dusk and disappear amid the grey skids of cloud.

I rang Khalid.

'Anto, my mate!'

'Howaya, what's the craic?'

'Oh – none – packing.'

'Packing? For where?'

'I'm going home.'

'When?'

'After the exams. Next week. I'm sending my stuff over first, then I'm legging it to London for the summer.'

'Bollocks! I thought we'd hang out this summer!'

'Oh yeah?'

'Yeah! I was going to take you round all the gay bars and try to indulge your bi-curious side!'

'Oh?'

'Yeah, fuck it, I was gonna get you drunk and try to kiss you. Jesus, I'm so pissed off!'

'Don't be. It's cool.'

'But I was really looking forward to making you want me. Fucking *London* is stealing my new boyfriend!'

'Yeah, well,' Khalid said, 'if you really mean it, you'll just have to follow me over, won't you?'

41. Black or blue

I was stuck beside loud businessmen on the flight to London. It was a routine journey for them and their big bellies – G&Ts, bluffing about mergers, the embarrassing one-upmanship of uncles at weddings. Economy-class plane journeys are so *straight* – functional, a means to an end, depressing. Breeders have no style, and only a heterosexual man could have conceived such a one-size-fits-all experience: the perma-smile waitrons; the carpet on the seats and ceiling; the elbow-knocking discomfort that reminds you that the human need to actually, physically travel – to exist through time and space – is merely an inconvenience to those in the business of *renting seats*. Planes are just buses with disposable, pre-moistened hand-towels. Vile. When I'm a popstar, I'll be permanently trashed on premier-class vodka martinis, drunk enough to glance out the window and still be surprised to think, 'Wow! I'm airborne!'

I answered questions in my head that interviewers would ask when I was famous.

'So Anto, what looks do you currently favour in your fabulous Manhattan apartment?'

'Well Janet, I'm very influenced by minimalism – I admire the cool, uncluttered, efficient approach to life – though I must say, aeroplane food is an example of that philosophy brought a step too far, haha! But I like a touch of opulence to offset the white, streamlined perfection of my home, so I splashed out on reformatting an image from the photoshoot for our latest CD to cover one wall, yes, that's right, the single is called *Girls (You Know You Wanna)*, and you can buy it in chainstores and airports the whole world over right now!'

'How marvellous. So, do you have a boyfriend at the moment?'

'Golly, yeah, I do, though he gets a bit jealous what with all the groupies! No, I'm kidding, I think it's all about respect, you know? Lots of guys send me their underwear in the post, stuff like that, the charlady uses them to polish the silver. Well I *hope* she washes them first! Yeah, I'd like to say a big hello to my boyfriend, Khalid Kashani, the international football star – he's probably crying into his Tia Maria and milk right now, pondering the futility of life without me. Miss ya honey!'

'What a lucky boy. Do you have any words of advice for the legions of fans who are thronging the malls here in Tokyo just to catch a glimpse of you, Anto Broderick, idol and demi-god to a vast swathe of richly pocket-moneyed global youth?'

'Absolutely, I'd just like to remind my fabulous, gorgeous fans that the meaning of life is to be splendid, then die. The end!'

And so I daydreamed amid clouds until the plane brought me down to earth with a bump and I woke up, thrilled, at Heathrow.

Luggage thudding, English voices chirruping, a face in the crowd that's pleased to see you – I felt so generic, and wished the camera could slow down to record that moment where happiness seizes us enormously, in widescreen, in a sudden hush, in the connection between a pair of black and a pair of blue eyes – but life limps on around you, others crush and crowd and break the spell that held you together for a fraction of a second, and the moment can only be replayed in a loop across your bedroom ceiling when you're lonely.

42. Travelling light

Khalid gave me a quick half-hug.

'I like the new haircut! Good journey?'

'Shite.'

'You need to get your luggage?'

'Nope, this is it.'

'What? That's all?'

'Yeah.'

'That little bag?'

'Travelling light is very fabulous. Decko reckons I learned a lot from Sindy and her bijou suitcases.'

'What did you bring?'

'To wear?'

'Yeah. We have to co-ordinate when we hit the clubs. We have to look good together.'

'Oh, bla, my Diesel shirt, with the dragons. A couple of lo-fi TopMan T-shirts. The red vest-top, the one I was wearing that time when that weird fella kept asking me to sell him speed.'

'Do I have to get some gay tops?'

'Your tops are *all* gay, Khalid.'

'I have to get some straight-acting tops then. In a gay stylée.'

'Deal!'

On the tube, a sign said 'PLEASE DO NOT EAT SMELLY FOOD', with a picture of a curry. Was that racist?

I told Khalid about the other times I'd been to London. It had mostly been for dance competitions when I was younger – sequins, sweat and temper-tantrums – though I'd been over clubbing since with the lads, show-ing off our disco tits.

'Did you win anything?'

'I was in some groups that won stuff.'

'What was it like?'

'Bitchy. Girly. Really competitive, you know, amongst ourselves, I mean.'

'Were all the guys gay?'

'Most, eventually.'

'Are all gay men good dancers?'

'Oh, please. Have you seen the state of – no, you haven't. Yet. But you will. Let's just say, the best male dancers tend to be gay, but so do the worst. Mind you, straight guys don't even try.'

'I try.'

'I know.'

Mixed impressions: more grim-faced commuters than Dublin; more black and Asian faces than you'd see on British telly; quicker glances, an edge of menace and excitement that might just have been expectation. Londoners were more *drab* than you'd expect – I was the best-dressed guy I could see. I was chuffed to walk through the Underground with Khalid, both of us sneaking glances at each other and laughing at the mingers we effortlessly surpassed.

'Are you thinking what I'm thinking, Anthony?'

'I think I am, Khalid.'

'Hehehe!'

We each pinched a fat, womany arse-cheek of some besuited chap waddling ahead of us and ran in fits of giggles up the stairs to a thirsty freedom – the thin, grey air of cold, excellent London.

43. Coming home reminds you why you left

Khalid's home was a train-ride away, in the suburbs, where the shops and pubs melted in an attempt at leafy gentility that couldn't quite hide the graffiti on electrical boxes. Kids aped disaffection in black hoodies. Beige-clad neighbour-units scurried between car and front door, front door and car, as if the air that other people breathed might be tainted with the spores of alternative lifestyle choices. It was as easily recognizable a place as Mickey D's, at once both familiar and alien, a place where we could all agree to belong without any messy notions of emotional engagement. I'm sure it was rife with mutual loathing, just like anywhere.

The house was big – huge windows, massive rooms – with the slightly shabby air that only truly posh people get away with.

'Are we home alone?'

'Mum and Dad are at the theatre tonight, which is good. You're the first person I've ever taken home. Imagine! A little Irish gay boy for my first friend! They'll be worried.'

'Who cares? Don't you have any friends?'

'I can't bring Johnser home, he's Jewish. My brother Rick would kill me.'

'Eh, do I have to meet Rick?'

'Nah. He'll be seeing to business in the city. I'll show you his gym and his sauna. I'd let you try it out but someone might – catch us at it.'

The traditional Arabic sitting room was decked out in green and gold, with low chairs and sofas placed around the walls. A curved sword took pride of place.

'Deadly!'

Khalid split a fig between us.

'Ever had a fig before?'

'Nope.'

'What do you think?'

'Ugly on the outside. Pretty on the inside. Um, there's not much … taste to it.'

'It's supposed to symbolize the female sexual organs. Stories and fables go mad over them. I think they're overrated, myself.'

He played some cassettes that his parents had to import from home.

'I thought Irish reels were bad.'

'Could you do a dance routine to it?'

I improvised, and Khalid's sister caught us boogying around the kitchen. Scarlet!

'You must be Anto,' she said brightly, taking my hand from Khalid's waist and shaking it with a smile. 'I'm Lyla. How's the band?'

'Oh, it's cool. I'm normally better than that ...'

'I hope so. But you probably need someone more experienced than Khalid to practise with.'

'He's not so bad. I could break him in.'

'I bet you could. Well, boys, any plans for tonight?'

'A few. Uh, nothing definite,' Khalid said, straightening his clothes. 'Are Mum and Dad going to be back tonight?'

'Nah. I'll be in bed early, so don't wake me up when you stumble into bed.'

'Anto's in Rick's room,' Khalid said.

'Well, sure. Cool. Whatever. Nice to meet you, Anto. Have fun – I've got to study, finals in a week. Look after my baby brother, whatever you get up to!'

Lyla went off with a stack of notes clutched to her breast. Khalid made for the fridge.

'That was a close one. Come on, we'll sneak these up to my room. If Lyla asks, they're yours!'

We took the beer up to Khalid's very boyish bedroom – he had a football-motif border around his blue walls – and flopped on the floor to flip through his photos.

'I wasn't born here, I was born in Italy, but my parents moved when I was a few months old. Rick speaks some Italian. I didn't have a word of English when I first went to school. I sat there going "Ehhhhh?" all day.'

'You were a fat kid!'

'Ehhhhh?'

'You. Fatso. Hahaha!'

'I only acquired my manly physique quite recently. You know, we should go to the gym together in Dublin next year.'

'You think?'

'Yeah, I need a gym buddy.'

'We'll see how the band rehearsals go. So what was school like?'

'I picked up English gradually, I just had to, really. My mum still doesn't have great English. I was sent to an English school during the week and then an Islamic school on the Saturday, that's our holy day – well, every day is holy, but it's our Sabbath if you like – so, I was always at school and, like, nothing ever happened on a Sunday. I wasn't much good till my A-Levels, then I really put the work in. I wanted to get away. Start a new – start a new life in a new place. You know what I mean?'

'I'm still trying,' I said.

'You've got your band.'

'Big deal. We're not on telly! We've been going for ages, but because we're not as-seen-on-TV, we're no one. You're lucky you've got college.'

'Fuck it, I hate it. I've started doing ... promise you won't laugh?'

'No.'

'I'll tell you anyway, but don't tell anyone. I've started doing ... *ballroom dancing* classes. And writing poetry. Is that stupid?'

'I dunno. I'm in a boyband, that's pretty wussy.'

'You think I'm a wuss?'

'Do *you* think you're a wuss?'

'I don't want people to ... think ... I'm gay.'

'You've had girlfriends, haven't you?'

'Only one, before Jennifer. We broke up when I went to Trinity.'

'How long?'

'Six months, kind of thing. She was bossy.'

'Was she a bitch?'

'Yeah.'

'Are you sure you're not gay?'

'I'm not gay, man.'

'Yeah, but would you tell me if you were?'

'You'd – you'd be the first to know. I promise.'

I nodded. We drank. A motorbike backfired below us in the street, sending birds squawking past our window. I imagined sparks and birds alike exploding in the wake of clouded diesel, in shimmering stars that glowed for no time at all and vanished, like promises made to be broken.

44. Picture postcards (notes to self)

With any lazy holiday the sense of narrative is lost when you try to remember what you did each day. I guess, as modern creatures, we're not used to processing free time efficiently – we're more used to leisure being programmed into our daily schedule – and the brain recalls only picture postcards of certain moments, haphazard and vital for being orphans of duty.

Drinking Black Bull cocktails in Soho. Khalid declaring a faggy sales assistant 'one of us'. Being offered Es and speed in Camden. A crazy guy in Mickey D's being goaded into throwing his burger at some pissed-up knacker. All knackers drinking Stella on the tube. Finishing a lunchtime Guinness but leaving behind the meat pie. Khalid's mate looking me up and down over a snooker cue when I said I didn't play footie. A girl in Boots smiling at my 'i hate work' T-shirt. Seeing Alma from *Coronation Street*. Paying a tenner each (sterling!) to see some shitty blockbuster movie in the middle of the day, then sleeping through it. Talking till dawn in Khalid's brother's bed. Meeting Lyla and her gang unexpectedly in Prêt-à-Manger. Hopping on a double-decker bus while it was moving. Realizing everyone at our table was a different religion – Muslim, Catholic, Jewish, Buddhist.

The real stories happened in clubs – love stories, drug stories, stories of faith – the kind of stories where you don't even realize that your lives are flipping over, that the relationship between you and the guy you're falling in love with is changing, the kind of everyday stories that come to make or break a friendship.

45. Popstarz

There were the knackers, drinking Stella on the tube. It was as if an entire tribe from round our way had been teleported to London – same tracksuits, different accents. Knackers are universal. I didn't want to, but Khalid sat opposite them. I was too wary to talk much in front of them – faggots and blacks being the natural enemy of white trash – so Khalid's attempt at conversation fell to desultory monosyllabic answers. I listened and tried to make myself invisible.

One of the knackers (a really cute specimen I accidentally caught the eye of) hissed, 'He's wearing make-up!' but not loudly – just loud enough for one of the other guys to pick up the vibe and start some story about how a gay porno mag at the newsagents where he worked had fallen off the shelf (yeah, right) exposing many various aspects of gay sex to his horrified gaze. He'd obviously learned a lot, and described it in graphic detail to his mates who groaned in all the appropriate places. They seemed to enjoy being disgusted – I spotted at least one hard-on through silky white tracksuit bottoms – and by the time we hopped off at King's Cross, I had quite a mental checklist of activities I'd have liked to practise on Khalid that night.

'He saw your make-up, Khalid.'

'Shit. Did he think I was gay?'

'What do you expect?'

I'd done Khalid's make-up for him before we went out, robbing his sister's modest stash. Her skin-tone was darker though, so you could see it under harsh lights.

'I'll wash it off.'

'Leave it, it's cool.'

It was basic slap to cover up a slight outbreak of spots – 'First night nerves, man!'

'I don't want all the boys after me.'

'Of course you do. Oh Christ, look at the queue.'

'I gotta phone home.'

'Why?'

'Let Lyla know I'm out.'

'Does it matter?'

'It might. It won't take long. Anyway, that queue's not moving.'

We had to queue at the phone box though. (We didn't take our phones cos they spoiled the line of our jeans.) It was being used as a pick-up spot by a bunch of prostitutes and their pimps, all of whom were black, and I was glad to be with Khalid, the way they looked me up and down.

Duty done, we shivered in the queue for Popstarz – indie kids, skater boys, pop princesses – there was a good mix. Everyone else seemed to know one another. Khalid took my hand – 'Just in case they don't let me in!' – and once inside, we hit the bar for cheap lager and to check out the talent.

On the dancefloor, Khalid beamed. 'I think we've found our niche!'

I pretended not to hear him – after all, I couldn't snog my sister's ex, not when he'd spent half the day talking about how great she was – could I?

I feigned interest in a Morrissey lookalike, troubled that neither Khalid nor I would make the first move, not sure whether I should be worried that he might want to, or worried that he might not.

We took a breather in the Rubbish Room. Trashy pop – yay! When my back was turned, a skinny girl hopped my boyfriend (well, he *might* have been) with the excuse, 'I'm on a hen night, sorry!'

'Man, I always seem to get the girls on hen nights!'

'Yeah, well, you know why, don't you?'

'I'm irresistible?'

'They have to do dares. One dare is *always* to kiss a black guy. You're just a *type* to them.'

Khalid was a bit quiet after that, but talked about Jennifer all the way home in the taxi, even though his hand kept touching mine as I stared out the window, counting prostitutes in phone boxes.

46. Heaven

'Lowbrow is fine,' I said, 'it's honest. Highbrow is fine too, because it's the pinnacle of excellence. It's *middlebrows* I hate. People who think they're better then commoners but have no sense of fun and no sense of beauty.'

'I hate the middle classes,' Khalid said. 'They're the people who didn't like me or my family because we're black, or Muslim, or foreign, but decided we were OK when they found out we had money. It's nothing to *do* with money. I'm still treated as an underdog and I wouldn't want their quiet lives anyway. Racist, classist, *boring.*'

'And the middle-aged,' I added. 'Not an age, but an attitude. People who waste their whole life and regret it. Waking up and realizing you're jealous of mad homeless alcoholics because they're *free.*'

'There's no such thing as freedom,' Khalid said. 'You just gotta choose a prison you're happy with.'

We made each other feel so cool when we were high.

I used to save all my spite for kids who thought they were cool. I hated anyone with the right haircut, the best jeans, the flashiest trainers. I used to go barefoot in PE just to not fit in. I knew the destinies of those local teenage starlets – I knew they would all become middlebrow, middle-class, middle-aged losers, if they were lucky. I knew I had to be different, but somewhere along the line, somewhere between discovering other fags to hang out with and needing to get a half-proper job (just to tide me over on my path to superstardom, natch), I realized the strategic benefits of blending in. How adopting a mainstream uniform could be clever. How having the right haircut might not get you laid, but it would definitely put you on the 'potentially shaggable' list. Because, in truth, I never fancied people who were particularly different. Beautiful losers, sure. I guess I developed a love-hate relationship with ordinary boys. So, I learned how to brand myself as a sorted, happy gay boy whom you'd love to buy a pint for, whom you'd love to get to know better, whom you'd love to let join your squeaky-clean, mega-ambitious pop band. I found my tribe. We only want what everyone else does – money, recognition, sex and drugs of choice – but we want them upgraded, super-sized, harder, faster, better, more. We want to take your average life and expose its banality and comfort for fear. We want to do what you're scared to do and make it glamorous. We want to make perfection look easy and inspire envy in the sort of folk who reminisce endlessly about how great school was, way back when popularity meant tyranny, when they were the ruthless rulers of cool and we were the runts of the litter – with our lispy voices, immaculate grooming and singalong pop tunes. I want to look on with pride when Walter's gang of softies finally gets their revenge on Dennis the Menace.

We grabbed a quick bite to eat at Mickey D's ('one fart and it's gone') and joined the queue for Heaven. Lots of black guys, lots of muscle, one excited Anto and a Khalid more nervous than before.

'This is what I expected gay clubs to be like. Look at all the glitter! Man, we need to go to that gym.'

There were straight lads round the corner in the Square, a world away, fighting over curries in between trips to the ATM and the taxi rank. Our crowd were total queens, preeny, fabulous, catty, like they'd fuck you five times before breakfast and chuck you out on your skinny white ass if you suggested a coffee along with the cream.

Heaven is huge. We slid amongst the sweaty, glistening bodies. The downstairs music was relentless. The VIP area held a bevy of impossible drag queens sipping from someone's granny's china. The shop was selling clubwear, muscle tops, fetish gear …

'What do you think?'

'It's cool,' Khalid shouted. 'Let's take a walk.'

We wandered the club like two lost kids at a carnival. I got confused by my money at the bar – I think they thought I was a lying, cheating bastard – but we found the R'n'B room and relaxed. The crowd was mostly black, the music more soulful, more melodic. I still had to drag Khalid onto the dancefloor.

'You dance like a white guy!'

'Well, I'm a straight guy, how does that fit with your preconceived little notions?'

'Pretty badly.'

'Oh wow! Look at him! He's so cool!'

He was a bleach-blond tight-afro in pastel lipstick and eyeshadow.

I was outclassed.

'He's the coolest person here, we have to talk to him!'

'You talk to him, I'll be at the downstairs bar.'

I left Khalid to chat up his femme-bot, wondering if he really did prefer women. Or trannies. Or chicks with dicks. And could I compete?

Khalid found me just a few minutes later, drinking stubbornly in a chill-out booth.

'He wasn't that cool. He looked cool but he didn't have much to say for himself.'

'Did you snog him?'

'Nah! I didn't want to. You should chat him up ... or someone. You could have anyone here, anyone you wanted. You're so ... *charismatic*.'

'I don't want anyone.'

It felt like silence, although I suppose the music kept on thumping. I spaced out for a bit, and when I tuned in again, Khalid was being chatted up by a tall black guy in white tracksuit pants. The tall guy beckoned me over to talk to his mate, a big guy with dreads.

Preliminaries dealt with (Kevin, twenty-one, a dancer on a break because of an injured foot), Kevin jerked his thumb at Khalid and said, 'Your mate here's trying to tell my mate Jay that he's straight.'

'He is, Khalid's straight.'

'He is not.'

'He says he is.'

'Oh, come on. You're definitely gay, aren't you?'

'Oh yeah, totally.'

'So are we, and *hell-o*, I know a gay man when I see one. He is *not* straight, mate.'

'Well, I don't think so either. You know, I *think* he keeps flirting with me –'

'Do you like him?'

'Yeah, I guess.'

'He's cute.'

'Yeah. He used to go out with my sister though. We shared a bed last night –'

'Nice!'

'– and he wouldn't shut up about her.'

'Man, he's got issues.'

A little queen came bouncing up to Kevin, whisking him away – 'I'll be back, Anthony, see ya later! Yeah, definitely, man!' – and Jay turned my way.

'Tell me this guy isn't straight, mate.'

'He's straight. Sorry,' I said, and downed a slug of JD and Coke.

'He isn't, no way. What's your name?'

'Anthony.'

'Jay.'

We shook hands, the veins in Jay's arm straining against chunky bracelets.

'I know he's not straight,' I told Jay, 'but he's not even out to himself, I don't think.'

'So what's he doing here?'

'It's for my benefit, apparently.'

'I think he's enjoying it more.'

'Yeah, well, I don't know. I don't know if it's cos he's black, or Muslim, or if he's just your regular closet case and there's no real reason. He chatted up some bloke in make-up tonight and he still says he's straight.'

'You just need to be there for him, in case he needs a shoulder to cry on,' Jay grinned. 'Rather you than me, mate!'

One more tour. From the balcony, I watched the bodies swirl and mingle in kaleidoscopic patterns that hypnotized us into thinking we were all alike, all beautiful. I was full of love for every bastard, slut, shy boy, queen, every loser and every bit of rough – but I left with Khalid all the same, still at a loss. I'd been out for five years. Wasn't I supposed to know how to handle a new boy?

We decided that Heaven was a good place to visit, but we wouldn't want to live there. Chemicals crackled across the night air. Girls sang, buses heaved through the city, dramas were born, died, and resurrected endlessly because our lives were all the same. That didn't help when I was stuck beside a boy I so badly wanted to kiss, but had to wake up from his own sleepwalking sexuality before I could make him see he wanted me too. Obsession crawled across my skin and I shivered. Khalid draped his jacket over my shoulders and we huddled together, haloed in neon in the back of a taxi.

47. G.A.Y.

At the door, we were asked if we'd like to fill in a questionnaire to help the Gay Men's Health project better understand its clients' needs. The first question was:

What is your sexual orientation? (Please tick)

Gay
Bisexual
Man who has sex with men
Other (Please specify)

Khalid ticked 'Bisexual'. We filled it in quickly – I put in Khalid's London address as mine – and went for a slut strut on the dancefloor, to the bar, on the balcony. Big hair and day-glo was still in fashion. Tons of little headless chickens ran around squawking in the clouds of dry ice.

'There's a frigging chipstall!'

'Naff!'

Stubble was growing back on my shoulders. When Khalid's arm brushed mine, a little electric shock passed between us. We turned to each other, eyes wide, then smiled. Khalid closed his eyes. I looked at his face. It was calm, unreadable, his lips a little wet, his brow smooth and unworried. It was the perfect moment to lean in, kiss him ...

'Tequila!' he declared, snapping open his eyes. The moment was gone. He trotted off to the bar, for all the world like just another gay-boy, up for it in his vest-top and glitter at G.A.Y., the trashiest, poppiest, sleaziest, youngest club in London. It must have kept the Minogue sisters alive during their lean years.

We threw back the tequila. Khalid was mesmerized by one black bump'n'grinder dancing alone beside us near the bar.

'Look at that ass! Can you imagine having sex with that? Baby!'

I left him to it, bored of wondering what he was playing at. I ignored the older guys eyeing me up. I ignored the skinny schoolboys, most of whom hadn't outgrown their fag-hag friends yet. I tried to ignore the nagging little voice telling me, *Talk to Khalid! Ask him what he's at. Then hop on him!*

A few tequilas later, we were chilling out in the chill-out room.

'Do you consider yourself a good Muslim?'

'Yeah.'

'Even though you drink?'

'Well, I'm British, aren't I?'

'Even though you're hanging out in gay bars?'

Khalid shrugged.

'What's the Islamic stance on homosexuality?'

Khalid looked uncomfortable. 'Islam is a peaceful religion, you know. We get a bad press. It's not all bombs and bullets.'

'Yeah, I know that. There's extremists in any religion. But you can't be a good Muslim and be gay, can you?'

'I reckon, if you can't help it, then it can't be wrong, can it?'

If you can't help it. And if you were bisexual, did that mean you *could* help it?

'But do you actually believe all that God, eh, Allah stuff?'

'What?'

'Religion is all dogma. It's bullshit. It's only there to make you feel guilty about yourself, to make you sacrifice your life for the sake of an imaginary good place. Oh, I don't know how to explain it –'

'Don't disrespect my religion, man.'

'It's not *your* religion, I mean *any* religion. It's like the ultimate insurance scam. *Give us all your money, time and effort in this life, and we promise the next one will be better.* That's how it *began.* Jesus was the first icon, he was like the first rock star. I wish I had his PR company. The whole gay thing fucks up their theory that sex is for babies, full stop, so they try to suppress it.'

'Gay people still have babies. If I was gay, I'd still want kids.'

'Well, you shouldn't give up your whole life for them.'

'Life's not all about sex, either.'

'I'm talking about love. Gay people fall in love too, you know. Then religion comes along killing people for falling in love, it's disgusting. Everyone knows priests are all faggots or paedos anyway. It's fucking sad that gays were made to feel as bad as baby rapists, and that they had to, to *sublimate* their sexuality, to swear celibacy and go about preaching to people back in the real world about how to behave. I *despise* religion.'

'You disrespect my religion, you disrespect me.'

'If I don't respect my own religion why should I respect yours?'

He stalked off.

First I thought, *He's a drunken Muslim in a gay club, and he wants to argue religion with me?*

Then I wondered which of us had sounded more zealous. *But I only said it for his own good!* I felt … I'm not sure.

I felt an unfamiliar emotion.

I think it might have been shame.

48. Umbrellas unfurl like a million mushrooms

High above the city, umbrellas unfurl like a million mushrooms. From here, life flows in a pattern, mirroring the swirls of cloud that rain upon the streets below.

Aeroplanes rumble through imaginary flight paths. Birds trawl on a wavelength of their own. Moths seek light, but can never get close enough, because they're near blind, clumsy. If all the flying creatures mobilized, they could black out the sun, cut off the city from its lifesource, descend in the darkness and ravage, chasing the panic until it was an empty gloom. The flying creatures have the luxury of perspective, should they choose to use it.

I fall through the layers of air, through the smog, the dust, crash-landing in the alleyway behind the club. I don't wake up yet. I sink into the soft plastic bags that mother my sweaty head. I feel disconnected from my veins.

I wake up now. A day later. One hangover older. Drops of rain glint in Khalid's hair like constellations I have dragged from the slumbering sky.

49. His left eye is lazy

As Khalid stared out the window of the train, I found myself mesmerized by the laziness in his left eye. His good eye followed the flow of suburban concrete, his other trailed just a little out of synch, as if he was trying to focus on something no one else can see.

Maybe it can see through holes in time and space. Maybe, as we sit in mostly silence, maybe it jackknifes reality into what-might-have-been, into one of those parallel universes where we were something other than lost.

It started to rain. The window wept at us, and Khalid put his fingertips to the glass, adopting the pose of a poor kid staring at a toy he really wants for Christmas in a black-and-white movie.

'You know how to not get wet when it rains?'

'Stay inside?'

'Outside. You're not funny,' I said, and he smiled to himself.

'How then?'

'You brace yourself. You remind yourself that you're only atoms. If you walk steadily through the rain, ignoring it almost, and allow all your atoms to disconnect, you slide through the rain much faster than anyone watching you would realize. All the rain is just atoms too, and it falls mostly between your –'

'Like how pictures are broken up before they reach your telly?'

'Yeah, like that. And the atoms of rain are only static.'

It feels like an old train. The carriage shudders. Khalid turns away from the rain and stares me in the face, both eyes focusing on mine. He shakes his head, and he is perfectly serious.

50. Searching for the face of Jesus

Jesus was such a pansy. The nice guy. The celibate. The man's man with a handpicked gang of twelve Muscle Marys who followed him everywhere so they too could be 'fishers of men'. The devoted son. The peaceful political agitator. The man betrayed by a kiss. The puritan, the best friend, the naked victim who, in the end, blamed it all on his da and inspired a cult following of sexually tormented, psychotic, devout maniacs who wanted to save the whole world through high theatre and camp singalongs.

Religion is pantomime. It never would have caught on if Reality TV had been invented.

Even now, Jesus has a lot to answer for in the gay imagination. We may have lost our faith, but we're still looking for that one special guy to save us, to love us unconditionally, to tell us that we're OK, forever.

Jesus was the first superhero, the first nude pin-up, the first global brand. They sold him as a saviour, creating the blueprint for woe-is-me homo-suffering, while the rest of the world just wanted to party. Jesus, the other-worldly aesthete, who stood apart from the vulgar pleasures of the common crowd while his marketing department rewrote 'self-righteous denial' as 'moral superiority'.

Thank fuck Ecstasy replaced Communion.

51. The pyjama game

Ma and Da were rowing because Ma read an article about Female Emancipation and decided that It Just Wasn't Good Enough. I tried to butt in – 'Ma, feminism happened *decades* ago, it's too late to catch up!' – but they were enjoying themselves too much. When she started screaming about having the right to multiple orgasms Da got real excited, so I left them to it.

I met the lads down the pub to fill them in on all the London gossip.

'Sweetie, did you meet the parents?'

'Oh yeah. His ma was really nice and wore a sari thingy, it was embroidered, dead posh. His da was very proper and gave me this look that would cut you in two, I swear. I don't think I passed the marriage test.'

'We're not talking marriage, just a quick fumble to prove you were right about him. Right?'

'Hmm – not going to happen.'

'No?'

'Nah. I mean, I spent a whole night in bed with him – twice – and nothing happened.'

The lads just looked at each other.

'What?' I said.

'A whole night in bed?' Decko said.

'Twice?' Terry said.

'And nothing happened?' Connor said.

'Exactly,' I said.

'O-*kay*,' Connor said, 'but did you try anything on?'

'Like – oh, it's so hot, let's get the pyjamas off?' Decko suggested.

'You wear pyjamas? I don't wear pyjamas. He *certainly* didn't wear pyjamas.'

'I *like* pyjamas! Anyway, you know how – hang on, what *were* you wearing?'

'Boxers.'

'Both of you?'

'I think he wore a T-shirt, the first night.'

'Sweetie, *get the hint*!'

'No, he didn't want me to do anything!'

'But he *couldn't* make the first move, he's the straight one.'

'Hang on,' Decko said, 'aren't the straight ones supposed to make the first move? Treat the gay guy like a girl? I think I read that somewhere.'

'But he's a closet case,' Connor said, 'so I don't think that counts. I think he needed you to – take him in hand.' Cue sniggering all round. 'Sorry!'

'I don't know, he talked a lot about Jenny.'

'That's so *over*.'

'Did they have sex?'

'No!'

'There you go. He must be gay.'

'So what do I do about it?'

'Get him drunk and cop a feel.'

'Get him to stay over at yours this time.'

'I can't. Zak.'

'Oh yeah. Well, all the more incentive to get your own place.'

'You could always try Mr McGinnity's.'

'Too organized. Anyway, Mr McGinnity might want to join in.'

'Isn't he married?'

'Sweetie, don't even go there. Tell us more about the row. What did you do about it?'

'I apologized.'

The lads looked at each other again.

'What?' I said.

'You?' Decko said.

'Apologized?' Terry said.

'Voluntarily?' Connor said.

'Sure,' I said.

'Well,' Decko said, 'that's more than we ever get. It must be serious.'

'You can't argue with religion.'

'Did you ever find out the Muslim stance on homos?'

'I looked it up on the Net. It's a sin and all that, but they're really reluctant to punish it to the full extent of the law, in most places.'

'What's the punishment?'

'Eh, being squashed to death under a pile of bricks.'

'You serious?'

'Yeah. But normally there have to be six eye-witnesses.'

'Normally?'

'They … well the courts have been suspected of faking the evidence, sometimes. It's rare though. Most of the time they prefer to believe that there aren't any Muslim homos. Anyway, that doesn't apply to Britain, obviously.'

'What did his family make of you?'

'They were cool, I liked them. And he said that they said that I was welcome back. It's not a family problem, it's just him.'

'It's a family problem if he still fancies Jennifer.'

'Yeah,' I said glumly. 'I'll have to ask her what she thinks.'

'Don't tell her you slept with him.'

'Does he have a good body?'

'Not bad. He wants us to go to the gym together.'

'Well that settles it.'

'Fag.'

'Total fag.'

'Ooh! You'll be able to tell us if it's true what they say about bla –'

'Shut it!'

'Oh, please. He asks you all sorts of silly questions about gayers. I demand to know if he's well-hung!'

'I'll see what I can do. Purely in the interests of unscientific research, of course.'

'A toast – to Khalid's cock!'

'Long may it stand!'

On the way home, although preoccupied, I noticed a female junkie trying to beat up a bouncer at Spar, a man and a woman fucking in a phone box, and a pile of puke with blood speckled through it. Like the rest of the half-drunk civilians sliding along the city streets, I looked at none of these things twice.

52. Rugby for girls

'Cathy!' I hissed. 'You can't take Dunnes Stores bags into a gay bar!'

'I know, here, I'll hide them behind your armchair.'

'Hide them behind yours!'

'Oh, don't be silly, they're hidden – I saw that popstar chap the last time we were here and he was wearing a velour tracksuit, for goodness sake. Don't worry! You're still bee-yoo-ti-ful.'

'What the hell were you buying?' I asked, nosing in the brown paper bags, afraid of what I might see. 'I hope it's only tea-towels or something basic and domestically inclined. *That's* allowed, although you don't flash it all over town. Not in front of my potential husbands anyway.'

'Oh? What happened to Khalid?'

'Let's just say, he hasn't asked me to wear the veil yet, dammit.'

'I wonder if you'd get away with that?' Cathy mused. 'You could probably dress as a woman for *years* and get away with it. He could even have a real wife for making babies.'

'I'm not quite prepared to move to the Middle East. All that sun and sand would ruin my complexion. Cathy, are these clothes? I'm afraid to take them out in public. They're all *turquoise*.'

'Hideous, aren't they? I had to get twelve, seven for the girls and five for the boys, in all different sizes, why do men never wear –'

'But why?'

'For my rugby team,' Cathy said, with the insouciance of a socialite introducing her new sugar daddy.

'I'm going to the bar,' I said, 'and when I come back, *you* are going to explain why you've gone all butch. Ah!' I said, seeing the protest, 'Rugby is butch. You can't deny *that*.'

Cathy smiled sweetly – point taken! – so did this mean she was finally coming out? I doubted it. In some ways, Cathy was more firmly entrenched in the back of the closet than I suspected Khalid was (and she had some horrible dykey shoes she should have kept there with her). I mean, when she hung a k.d. lang poster above her bed, it was a big enough statement for her mom (and I mean 'mom', the woman *bakes*) to take her aside for a little chat about the birds and the birds. Her da, despite being a misanthropic petit-bourgeois equal-opportunities bigot declared it 'perfectly acceptable' for a child of his to be gay. ('It's those bisexuals I *really* hate.') Both of her ex-boyfriends have turned out to be screaming nellies (one is a nurse and the other looks like a weather-girl). She openly ogles women on the street, in bars, in cafés, on the telly and in Cosmo (which has a very high count of naked breasts, apparently). You would think that by now she would've just bought herself a set of power-tools and thrown away her razor, but no – 'I'm a model, I can't be a lesbian. And if I was, who'd want to be treated by a lesbian doctor?'

'Straight men?' I'd guessed, but she was having none of it. My point being, Cathy had tonnes of support – encouragement even – but just couldn't bring herself to say, 'I am gay.' I reckoned it would take another few years before the lesbian moments started adding up to one big lesbian revelation. Until then, it seemed that an aggressively male sport was going to relieve the sexual tension.

'So what's all this about rugby?' I asked, slipping a nice, tongue-loosening G&T under Cathy's delectable nose.

'It's through college. The meds have an official rugby team, of course, but we're like the comedy challenge team. It's all supposed to increase sociability and maybe find the girls a husband.'

'Bruises all over and broken noses? No thanks.'

'Everyone else is doing something. Trisha is working with Aids patients, Decko's doing yoga and Marsha's joined the born-again Christians.'

'What if you get injured and your modelling career goes wack?'

'Eff the modelling, it's not a career. All those skinny girls smoking their heads off, not one of them is really the *least* bit attractive. The rugby girls are more fit, and probably more *available*. Oh dear, was that a lesbian moment?'

Cathy giggled and I smiled indulgently, thinking that maybe this time Cathy would find her tribe. I tapped the bottom of my glass with a coin to re-inject some fizz, and drank to Cathy's new teammates.

53. Your phone is not your friend

The late shift on a Friday always brings out the freaks. I had one woman who rang up looking for a number in RTÉ and ended up lecturing me for forty-three minutes on the importance of maintaining a good relationship with my da.

'Me and my father used to go for a pint every Friday night when I finished work. Would you believe that?'

'Really?'

'He so enjoyed our little chats, now would you ever do that with your father?'

'Well, ha, no.'

'Perhaps you should!'

I ended up promising the lady I'd try to get my *father* to 'open up' over a pint of Guinness sometime soon, just to get her off the phone. Calls are meant to be wrapped up inside a minute max, and I kept reminding her that the call would cost a fortune, but I think she was on a one-woman mission to replace her Friday-night bonding sessions with a nationwide upsweep in father-appreciation. My da would run a mile (definitely a mile, he hasn't got used to kilometres yet, never mind homosexuals) if I tried to talk to him. He'd only think I was trying to talk about sex in a misguided attempt to make him 'understand'. Why would I bother? We're both much happier pretending we live in different Irelands, preferably on different planets, in mutually exclusive universes. It's a surprisingly achievable arrangement.

Decko and I took a break to swap our freak-of-the-night stories. The machine coughed up our made-to-order-hot-beverages-of-choice and I snuck open a window to blow smoke out into the sterile air.

'I had a guy who was looking for a sex-line.'

'Some sad loser?'

'Some guy at a party. I told him we didn't provide those sorts of numbers and he asked if *I* could provide for the burning desire of his sexual fantasies.'

'No! What did you say?'

'I said sure. He was pretty tame though. I think I scared him with my lusty intonations.'

You have to make your breaks real short on the late shift cos there's only ever four chronic losers working it at a time. The few computers breathing called us back to work, to draw one more freak out of the woodwork that night – me.

'Good evening, directory enquiries, what address please?'

'Eh, I'm looking for the number of, for, to, eh, Gubu. The pub.'

'No problem. Would you like to be connected?'

'No thanks, just the number.'

'Sure, just bear with me a moment.'

The number was onscreen but I wanted to play with my customer for a little bit longer.

'So, what's the pub like?'

'What?'

'Gubu, is it good?'

'Eh, well, it's OK, yeah.' He sounded suspicious.

'It's just I haven't been in ages, not since The Front Lounge was done up.'

'Oh! Really? No, it's still good, it's a laugh.'

'Do you go there a lot?'

'Ah, the odd time. I go more to Yello now, you know?'

'Yeah, Yello's nice. Are you going out tonight?'

'Yeah, yeah, I am. I'm going to Gubu, me and a few of the lads.'

'Right, here we are.' I gave him the number and added, 'Have a good time! Some of us are stuck here in work.'

'Are you working late?'

'Well, I'll be finished in half an hour. It's a drag. I'll be glad to get out of here.'

'You know, eh – what's your name?'

'John.'

'You know John, you should come on down here after work for the laugh, what d'ya think?'

'I dunno, maybe I will. What's your name?'

'Liam. I'm kind of short, in, eh, New Rock boots. Short hair, earring.'

'Well, if I'm there, I'll look out for ya. See ya later, Liam!'

'Yeah John, I hope so!'

Hehehe!

We clocked off half an hour later.

'Fancy a pint?'

'I'm wrecked, I just want to get home to my peppermint foot scrub. That sex talk left me drained!'

'What if I said … I had a date?'

'Since when?'

'Since half an hour ago when the lovely Liam rang looking for the number of Gubu.'

'Scandalous! The last time I was there, I found some guy's underwear in the toilets!'

'Ah well, we'll go for the laugh. See what happens!'

There was a full moon. It glowed across the decorative lake, the sculpted greenery and the buildings that slept standing up, one eye open to the city. A thin sliver of light slid through the scene like the thread of silver through paper money.

'What did he sound like?'

'Young, but like he might have a moustache.'

'Did you tell him your name?'

'I'm John.'

'One pint only, John.'

'Oh, don't be such a Cathy!'

The Liffey heaved like a river of puke. We passed another gay bar on the way, the small crowd of smokers eyeing us up. It had been years since we'd been there – way back before The George had been reclaimed from the corner-dwelling crotch-scratchers who frequented it then – and a number of queasy teenage memories regurgitated themselves as we stepped past the determinedly old-fashioned door.

'I had my first real snog in there!'

'Remember when Abi was threatened by an ex-con? In the toilets? With a knife?'

'And the guy who went apeshit when you stole his cigarettes?'

'I only borrowed them for someone else.'

'And the first time we took Cathy there and she said out loud that she couldn't be a lesbian because she wasn't fat and ugly?'

'Oh God, I bawled in a corner over some fella! How *Brookside*!'

'You still wanna go to Gubu?'

'We'll stick our noses in.'

We skulled one pint and legged it. There was no one cute in New Rock boots.

It turned midnight as I got home.

Khalid's birthday.

```
abc              301/1
Happy 19 th! I left
London way
hungover, soz 4
being on such a
downer! It's ur
last chance 4 a
global teen
rampage – hope
the next year is
one 2 regret!
Axxx
       Options
```

I got the reply just a few minutes later, while I decanted my Gubu pint down the pisser.

```
BEACH PARTY IN
SPAIN – WISH U
WERE QUEER –
BUT COULD U
HANDLE THE
HEAT ?
       Options
```

It was almost enough to make me wish I'd found Liam – but no.

54. Another pointless Sunday

It was supposed to be a Sunday – big fat dinner, Ma hassling us about not going to Mass, Da asleep under the *Sunday World* – but Emily, my older sister, swept back into our lives in a timeless whirl of tears and a cocktail dress.

'The wedding's off!' she screeched. 'Trev dumped – I dumped Trev!'

I raised my most sardonic eyebrow in a tribute to the louche queers of 1950s movies. 'I didn't know you were engaged.'

'Well we *should* have been! We *would* have been, eventually. Five years, the bastard! He has some tall blonde *tramp* laughing at his jokes now, the *fucker*!'

Ma and Jennifer (who comes home every Sunday cos she's holy, and usually hungover) rallied round; Zak promised to break Trev's face; Da woke up and tut-tutted and shook his head and actually seemed to *care*. He must have been relying on Emily for his first dose of respectable grandchildren. When I threatened to spawn some with a turkey-baster and a willing womb, the poor man didn't know what I was on about. I'd never seen him so confused, at least, not since the time I had to explain to him that women who live together tend to have synchronized periods.

Personally, I would have swept up Emily's broken heart into a pan and dumped it in a bin marked 'I told you so', but once Wedding Fever has hit the heteros you just can't shake sense into them, poor foolish creatures.

'Do you think she's pregnant?' Jennifer asked me in a whisper. 'I don't want to ask in case she's just got fat.'

'I *didn't* think so, till you mentioned it.'

Emily went to throw up and we looked at each other significantly.

'Love, tell us all about it. Zak, make your sister a cup of tea. Oh, love, it's awful, what happened?'

'It's only the usual,' Emily gulped. 'It's so common! I'm mortified. He met this *slut* in work and because he had money and because he had a girlfriend she had to have him!'

'Isn't that how *you* met Trev?' I asked innocently.

'*That* girlfriend turned out to be a fucking dyke! No offence. I loved him! Oh, my heart's broke …'

I'd been to school with Trev. He'd always been a bit of a toe-rag with women, but very generously used to get a lot of blokes extremely drunk, every weekend. Nice guy, natch.

'I'm raging!' Emily yelled, sequins flashing angrily across her bosom. 'If he thinks he's getting away with this – *ooh*! I helped him decorate his new flat, the bollix! She's shagging him right now, on *my* carpet!'

'He'll regret it,' Jennifer said. 'Mark my words. Now the main thing is that you're OK. Do you feel well, Em? How's your head? How's your tummy?'

'I'm not fucking *pregnant*, Jennifer, OK?'

'I didn't mean –'

'Yes you did. Jesus, I'm not *stupid*. I bet you don't remind Anto to go to the clap clinic.'

'She does, actually.'

'Well I hope you tell her to mind her own business! At least we're not shagging suicide bombers.'

'What?' Ma said, bewildered.

'She's delirious,' Jennifer said hastily. 'Zak, where's that tea? That'll calm her down.'

'Oh Ma!' Emily rambled, oblivious. 'We were gonna have a girl and name her after *you*! We were gonna open a pub and name it after Da! Oh Ma, we had such *dreams*!'

'Here's your tea.'

'Thanks, Zak,' Emily slurped.

'Do you want me to send him a computer virus?' Zak asked.

'Yeah, go on.'

'That'll wreck his e-business!'

'Drugs?' Da yelped, leaping up from his armchair.

Yadda, yadda.

I went for a smoke on the stairs, wondering why women had to marry their way out of despair, when it always left them broken-hearted. I passed the time till the tears calmed down by counting the lumps of chunky veg in the vomit-platter someone had left in the corridor. By the contents of the stomach spilled in our communal doorway, I judged the owner chronically undernourished.

55. The boy in Spar

I flicked through some magazines while Decko waited in line to buy some ice cream behind a gang of thieving six-year-olds, a homeless alcoholic with pockets full of change and a kid in a baseball cap who was buying top-shelf porn (the kind they put beside gay lifestyle magazines). There weren't enough celebrity hairstyles in women's weeklies any more – too many boring pics of celebrity babies. Since when was breeding *in*? Didn't the celebs know that all our little council kids would be trying for a cut-price designer baby of their own, named after the real thing, or the exotic location where the foetus was spawned?

'Ma, I've had twins! One's called Jordan and the other's called Bus Stop!'

I shoved the glossies back on the rack, disgusted at their abandoning of old-fashioned glamour. The eejits were supposed to make us jealous of their bodies, not squash them out of shape for the sake of baby dumplings! We were never meant to see celeb-husbands with bags under their eyes, buying disposable nappies and sleeping pills at some mangy all-night chemist! They were meant to chase immortality through the camera lens, not *offspring*!

Another chap in a baseball cap nudged me in the ribs.

'Here, what d'ya think of her?'

A generic blonde with big tits invited me to lick her cheap, well-thumbed centrefold.

'She looks like a right slapper.'

'Would you do her?'

'No.'

'Eh, but you're eh, aren't ya, ya know?'

'What?'

His baseball cap looked me up and down.

'You're bent, aren't ya?'

'Am I?'

'Ah, it's alright with me bud, it's nothin' to be ashamed of, I'm just *sayin'*. Me uncle's, ah, ya know.' Sniff. 'Me uncle's queer.'

'Eh, right.'

'Yeah. At least you're not ashamed to say it, ya know, me uncle's not either, ya know, he's sound. Ah, yeah. Good luck, bud!'

He stuttered off round by the breakfast cereals and Decko entered, stage right.

'Who's your friend?' he said. 'He's *cute*.'

We giggled out into the sun, leaving the baseball cap blushing by the Pop Tarts.

'Have you ever sucked cock to Eminem?' I asked.

'No way! That's a disgrace. That's sleeping with the enemy. I'd suck *his* cock, though.'

'I find it empowering.'

'Speaking of empowering, it's nearly Pride. You know what that means.'

'Yeah,' I said gloomily. 'Lesbian poetry.'

56. Anto's guide to hair for beginners (for Rock)

Like it or not, your **appearance** is how people first **judge** you. Sometimes you get to show your fabulous naked body to complete strangers in a sauna, but most of the time your **style** will be people's first clue to who you are and how you want others to see you.

You don't get to choose your body: your height, your build, your face. But you do get to choose how to make the most of what you have, which is what your sense of **style** should be all about.

First and foremost: **HAIR**

Your hair is your tribe. Hair is important because it instantly reveals your state of mind.

You want to look **cool**.

Clean, styled and funky hair equals a clean, styled and funky lover!

OK, I'm not saying you should groom your pubic hair (though some people swear by a shaven scrotum) but you have to realize that **Good Hair** is all about the availability of **Good Sex**.

Do not underestimate the hair!

It is the quickest way to judge how clued-in someone is. A **fashionable** haircut shows that you're an **up-to-speed** gay-boy, i.e. that you're **in the know**. Being **in the know** makes you **one of us**, and therefore means that you're **on the same wavelength**, which in turn makes you **shaggable**.

(Likewise, if you have **Bad Hair**, you are most definitely **clueless** and **unshaggable**.)

So what is Good Hair?

Good Hair is clean, shiny and always groomed. You do not have to conform to the latest hair trend – it is OK to have a signature look.

But some hair is beyond the pale!

Never have a **bowl haircut**: it doesn't suit anyone and will only attract sleazy old men who secretly want to be priests so they can abuse pageboys.

Never have a **mullet**: this is the reserve of OTT gay twats, lesbians and inbred rednecks.

As a rule, **Big Hair** is **Bad** (unless it's an afro, which can be quite cool!)
As with most things in life:

Keep it simple!

Short hair suits most men best.

Invest in a good cut.

You can't go wrong with short back and sides.

You will need to use a **styling product**, e.g. wax or gel. This tidies your hair, though don't overdo it or you'll look like a hairdresser.

So what sort of hair do you want?

Examples of Good Hair:

1. The Flicked Fringe

Number two back and sides, short on top. Smooth hair and flick fringe upwards with wax or gel. A classic.

—*suits everybody*

—*utterly functional*, if not exciting

—*takes about 2 seconds*, so excellent if you're pressed for time

2. Messy

Number two back and sides, short-to-medium on top. Work wax or gel through hair roughly, plucking little bits upwards randomly (or pseudo-randomly).

—*just-out-of-bed look* implies *sexiness*

—*doesn't have to be 'perfect'* – some spontaneity means if it gets a bit wrecked, it can still look good

—you can keep this look *between the newly cut stage and your next haircut* – varying lengths over time means your hair will evolve without effort!

3. The Suedehead

Number one or number two all over. Works best if you are

a) absolutely gorgeous, or

b) balding rapidly

4. The Fin

Short at back and sides, longer on top. Drag hair upwards between palms with strong gel. May need hairspray.

—best attempted if you are *cool and confident*, otherwise you'll look like a prat

—*very gay*, thanks to Beckham (and not your man out of Travis)

5. The Sidesweep

Longish fringe, shorter at sides, often a little funky at the back.

—*indie credibility* will be yours

—*difficult to do right!* doesn't suit everyone and you will need a stylist to do it properly

—*suffer the inbetween stage!*

These are the basic looks you should aim for.

If you want **highlights**, get them done professionally and be prepared to **pay good money**.

Dramatic changes of hair colour are usually disastrous (though I like English Pillar-Box Red, or Alien Blue). If in doubt, or if it all goes horribly wrong, **dye it brown**.

Personally, I think cosmetic surgery should be compulsory for all mingers. Until that glorious day, **take charge of your hair** and **maximize your attractiveness**!

57. Peaches

I love eating peaches straight from the tin. The juice runs down your face and through your fingers. Messy and sweet, like at our party, when I bought enough extra beer to pack Ma and Da off to his sister's for the night. Emily bought three different flavours of vodka and we got stuck in early, dancing in the windows, cranking up the music to show all the telly-addicts how much fun we were having. Khalid got the most pissed, after me. He was chucking shots down him like a man on a mission. I was hoping that mission was me.

'This one's lemon! This one's orange!'

When we polished off the vodka and Jennifer had passed out after trying on Emily's new bodice, we cracked open the Peach Schnapps Suzie had brought. Khalid told one of his stupid stories.

'My mate Steve, he never pulls. He gets snogs alright, but his birds never come home with him.'

I notice his cute little 'wiv 'im' accent more when we're drunk.

'We were walking home one night, and he sez, snogs! I don't need snogs! I want sex! I'm never gonna get a shag, man, I'm gonna die a virgin! And I sez, snogs is alright. And he sez, if I wanted snogs, I might as well – eat a peach!'

'To snogs!' I yelled, and we toasted snogs with a shot of Peach Schnapps. The syrup from the tins is yummier though.

Khalid started waving his money around, for no good reason other than he had it. Suzie snatched a hundred from his hand.

'I'll dance for your money,' I said. Suzie shoved the hundred down my keks.

'Man! That's my money!'

'If you want it, you gotta come and get it!'

He chased me around for a bit, but every time he shoved his hand down my keks, he missed the money by a long shot.

A sober-ish Decko put a comatose Jennifer to bed. I snogged Ferdy again – it's something that happens when one of us is drunk. Emily told us all about Trev's 'tiny dick'. I had to correct her. Not on Trev's size – we'd had showers together so I could confirm his tininess – but her categorization was flawed.

'Willy is small, dick is average, cock is *huge*!'

I ended up draped across Terry, Khalid and Emily on the sofa, Khalid absent-mindedly stroking my hard-on.

'Sweetie! Get a room!'

I dragged Khalid off to the bathroom.

'We got to talk,' I said, when the door was locked.

'We don't have to talk. I want my money shot – man! Are they your balls – or is that – a *peach*?'

Right there, in my bathroom, with Khalid's hand weighing up my balls and only the smell of drink between our lips, I burst into tears.

I know what his mate Steve meant about peaches. And if I wanted someone to talk to, someone to understand, someone I could get on with – I might as well have a *girlfriend*.

58. A chorus-line of closets, singing

I woke up drunk, stumbled into the shower, felt sad that my fabulous body was going to waste, wondered who had put me to bed, tried to forget what had happened with Khalid, failed, crouched under the water and almost fell asleep, dried myself roughly to the drumbeat in my head, walked around, saw that someone had cleared up the mess and crawled back into bed.

'The state of you,' Zak said. 'Put on some clothes and make me breakfast.'

'Can't face food.'

'Have a poo, you'll feel better. Then go make me a fry.'

'Alright.'

'Anto, you're a *mess*. Sort out your hair, and your *life*.'

I stumbled back to the bathroom, saw that I was indeed a mess, wondered which of my bad hair and crap life was the root cause of the other. Grateful for Zak's sound advice, I made him breakfast and drank a bucket or two of water. Zak said something about Da coming back before football practice and I went outside for a smoke.

I sat in the wan sunlight, thinking *Zak's got it sussed*. He didn't drink, didn't smoke, didn't chase men and then somehow didn't snog them when he had the chance … Birds swam in the air. Kids tried to kill each other. Mr McGinnity tiptoed over to ask me a favour.

'Anto, I need some advice and I think you're the man for the job. Can you come inside a moment?'

'Sure. But I'm hungover to fuck, so don't trust my judgment.'

Mr McGinnity chuckled and I followed his waddle into his ground-floor flat. The light inside had the quality of cold tea. It was faintly musty, not unclean, but you could feel the years of fading photo-albums, Mass cards, bric-a-brac and religious propaganda bearing down on you. The wallpaper, carpets and furniture were heavy, dark and floral. Fussy lace doilies covered occasional tables and the edges of the chairs and sofa. I had a sudden memory of boiled sweets and red lemonade.

Mrs McGinnity was watching *Telly Bingo*. 'That Shirley Temple Bar's got far too posh lookin'!' she announced. 'Hello, Anto. I haven't seen you in many's a long year inside this house. How's the form?'

'Hungover.'

'Good, good. Maurice'll make you a nice cup of tea, won't you, Maurice?'

'Certainly.'

Mr McGinnity pottered about the little kitchen while Mrs McGinnity ticked off her Bingo numbers, sucking Maltesers with a cup of tea that smelled suspiciously of Jameson's.

'Sugar?'

'Lots, thanks.'

'There you go now!' Looking pleased with himself, Mr McGinnity presented me with a dainty patterned cup on a saucer with a Chocolate Finger on the side.

'I'm not a fan of the Chocolate Finger myself, but Maggie has a taste for that sort of thing,' Mr McGinnity said with a broad wink.

Tea came out my nose in alarm, but when I looked up again, snorting with embarrassment, *Maurice* looked perfectly innocent.

'So Anto,' he said brightly, false teeth gleaming, 'how are *you*?'

I don't know why, but I told him about Khalid.

He nodded sympathetically.

'Well!' he said when I finished the bit about the bathroom. 'You should have just kissed him!'

'I know, I know …'

'No use crying over unspilled milk,' he said with another awful wink. I *think* I knew what he was on about, and guessed it must have been a witty thing to say about 500 years ago. 'For all you boys have come so far, you still have a lot to learn about love!'

'It's not love!' I said defensively. 'I'd be quite happy to shag him, break his heart and leave him for dead!'

Mr McGinnity just chuckled. 'Yeah, right. You know, you don't need to be hung up on acting, well, like such a *man*, Anto. It's OK to like someone and tell them as much.'

'No it's not,' I muttered. 'It's soppy.'

'Gay boys these days!' Mr McGinnity sighed. 'You've won the right to sex but it seems to me you still have to learn about self-esteem. Fifty years ago, my homosexual friends were proud to be different – they revelled in it, it was their *weapon*. Now, you all just try to emulate straight men, and believe me, we're not the best role models for a lad like you!' Mr McGinnity sucked his Chocolate Finger primly. This was too ridiculous. I laughed.

'Maurice, *darling*,' I drawled, 'you're not trying to tell me that you're *straight*.'

'Yes he bloody well is!' his missus yelled from her armchair.

'One might say Maggie wears the britches,' Mr McGinnity said. 'Which rather brings me to the point. I have, eh, a little *personal* favour to ask, young fella, if you're willing?'

'You're not going to ask me to spank you, or something?'

'Guess again.'

'Tie you up? Pee on your face? It's not *gerbils*, is it?'

'No, no, and no! Ha ha! No, it's nothing *seedy*. I have quite enough seed of my own.' Cue naughty wink.

'Come on then. Shoot.'

'Follow me!'

Mrs McGinnity smiled at us indulgently, Bingo book in hand, Shirley on the telly, as he led me to their spare bedroom. It smelled of vanilla. The blinds were closed. Mr McGinnity flicked the light-switch.

'Your potential boudoir, should you ever need it. Don't let the mirrors put you off.'

A long, mirrored sliding wardrobe filled one wall. The only other thing in the dazzlingly white room was a good-sized bed with hot pink silk sheets.

'Eh, yeah, cheers. Very, yeah, generous … of you. Eh, to …'

Mr McGinnity swept across the room and slid a wardrobe door aside with a dramatic flick of the wrist. It gaped and so did I.

'Which do you think?'

Mr McGinnity twirled, holding aloft two gowns he'd dragged from a fat rack of flouncy, bouncy, sumptuous style that pouted from the closet like a line of chorus girls. He fluttered his lashes, the dresses caressing either side of his pinkish face. 'The blue matches my eyes, but the yellow is rather daring, don't you think?'

I was appalled. I've always wanted to wear yellow and it just doesn't suit me – but it looked kind of … *fetching* on Mr McGinnity. The lucky old sod!

'How should I know?' I said. 'It all depends on your wig and your *shoes*.'

59. Grazed knees

I broke into song on the way up our stairs. The scabby walls echoed with my own backing vocals. Brown bare legs jutted round the corner. I stopped.

'That's some tune. One of yours?'

'Yeah.'

I faced him – Cathal. He was in his G.A.A. kit, leaning back across the steps, his head resting on his sports bag. He was looking at me through narrow eyes. His hair and face were sweaty.

'Sing me some more,' he said. 'Cheer me up.'

'What's wrong?'

'Not a thing in the world.'

'I don't feel much like singing.'

'How come?'

'You look terrible.'

'What do you care?' he said, suddenly angry.

'Fine. I don't.'

'Good.'

I went to pass, but Cathal sprawled his legs wide to stop me.

'Don't be such a dick, let me past.'

His knuckly hands dangled from his knees. Red hair curled between his thighs. He wetted his lips.

'You're pissed. Aren't you?'

He laughed. 'Not enough.'

'Bullshit. Are you supposed to be at training?'

He shook his head dumbly.

'Why not?'

'Didn't your da tell you? Didn't he even say?'

'We don't talk about you over dinner.'

'Yeah. I suppose not.' He stared at his hands, turned them palms up. A line of drool leaked over his lips.

'What's *wrong* with you?' I shouted, disgusted.

'M'ff d'tim.'

126

'What?'

'I'm *off* the *team!*'

'Bullshit. You're just pissed.'

'That's *why*. That's – fucking …'

He cried. Bubbles of snot, cider breath, the works. He pushed his hands into his face and shuddered behind wet fingers.

I used to like him, I thought. I knelt down on the bottom step, one hand on his shoulder. His legs wrapped around me lightly.

'Anto –'

From above, someone swore. We both flew apart and looked up. Cathal shoved me away, his snot and tears smeared across my face.

'Fuck off, you faggot! Get the fuck away from me!' he barked, pushing past, legging it.

My da stared down. He looked scared.

I hurled Cathal's sports bag over the railings. 'Fuck you too, bitch!' His bag crashed on his skull with a tinny clang, and he howled.

60. Kiss catch

I took Khalid out to get rotten drunk even though I knew it was a bad idea. We swung around bars, dancing, stupid, and there was only one way the night could go. We stayed out as late as we could, neither of us wanting to crush the glittering idiocy we'd sculpted from ourselves, both of us knowing – I'm sure of it – that one of us would throw in his hand. Over a greasy kebab (a nice British touch), Khalid said, 'You might as well come back to mine, it's closer.'

I said, 'Sure.'

Running through traffic, Khalid grabbed my hand – clammy. Lonely shadows hung in lit windows like angels watching us through the gloom. Breathless, we crept into his apartment, clumsy and loud, trying too hard not to wake up his flatmates.

'The sofa's quite comfy.'

'Can't I hop into bed?'

Pause. 'OK.'

We undressed back to back and I slid into bed. The sheets were cool. I tried not to take up too much space. When Khalid slid in beside me, even though he had done it before, it felt different – or I felt different.

Silence.

I didn't want to touch his body – I couldn't.

Then –

'I'm going to kiss you,' I said.

'No,' he said.

'Come on. Once.'

'Go to sleep.'

'But I know you want to.'

'You're drunk, just go to sleep.'

I tried to tell him that he'd led me on. I tried to tell him that everyone thought he was gay. I tried to tell him I could help, but he just said, *go to sleep, go to sleep, man, go to sleep* …

'You know what I'm gonna do?'

'Go to sleep?'

'I'm gonna make you a coming-out guide. I'm gonna write one just for you.'

Hesitating, he said, 'I'll read it.'

'Promise?'

'It'll be interesting. I *will* read it.'

'Khalid?'

'Go to sleep.'

'Can I hold your hand?'

'Go to sleep.'

'I've held it before.'

'Go to sleep.'

'Please?'

'No.'

And that was that.

I woke up far too early. I didn't dare open my eyes, breathe too hard or move. I waited till he roused himself, dressed slowly and stumbled to the bathroom. The room was rank with vodka sweat. I slipped off my keks, praying to a god that didn't exist that my hard-on would fade, and slipped on a clean pair I'd stashed in my jacket. I slipped last night's (slightly damp) underwear in my jacket pocket and stood up to dress. Khalid came in, clocked my too-tight new keks, opened his mouth to speak, thought better of it – *I would've just thought he was leading me on.*

We acted as if nothing had happened. I walked him to Trinity, he had some reason to go. We did the palm-knuckle-thumb shake – 'See you soon, man' – lingering a little too long on our goodbye.

'Yeah,' I said and turned away.

The morning was colourless, cold, and somehow the very sort of morning I associate with school. Too clean. Too bright. Too early. The clouds were the colour of chalk dust, the sky as white as if it didn't exist.

We didn't exactly fall out, not exactly. We just kind of avoided each other for a bit after that.

61. Reality check

Zak was watching a match in our room, eating cheesy crisps that smelled like his feet. I flipped the mousetrap, reset it, flipped it again. Zak threw a crisp at me. I laid it as bait in the mousetrap.

'Can't you watch that with Ma and Da?'

'Too much noise.'

I found myself in the kitchen, made a cup of tea, threw the tea-bag out the window and saw it splat with a satisfyingly wet fart on the grimy pavement four stories below. The pavement was only there to separate us from the iron railings, and to chuck things on. It housed a little stash of crappy litter – a bald hairbrush, a bit of a kid's old trike, some syringes, faded wrappers, mushy paper, unidentifiable nubs of plastic and shards of metal. Beyond, a limb of city, bandaged in terraced housing, slung with wire, bolted with solid lumps of officious building blocks, stabbed with spires like accusatory knifepoints from the centre of the earth.

Ma and Da were shouting at the telly. It's always like that when a match is on.

'Referee, ya bollix!'

'Jaysus, that was no foul!'

'If he'd learn to pass –'

'If he'd mark his man –'

'It's a holy fuckin' disgrace!'

Ma and Da have known each other since they were five. They went through every class at school together, ragging each other, tormenting their teachers with their fights, surprising no one when they started 'doing a steady line' at fifteen, put a ring on the finger at twenty-one, got hitched at twenty-two. You can follow their progress through little square photos that start off black-and-white but blend into sepia and cartoon colour. Scabbed knees, cheap toys, lurid furniture and acres of wall behind tiny little dots of smiles. First Holy Communion outfits and gappy teeth, like already battle-scarred mini-marriages. With cousins and brothers and sisters in front of parked cars. Together, with an engagement ring flashing on Ma's hand, her looking demure and amused, him grinning and chuffed in funky sideburns. The wedding, then babies, then nothing, except other people's weddings.

Ma and Da were each other's first and only girlfriend and boyfriend. What had they ever wanted, or expected? He went into labouring, she went into labour, he trained footballers, she trained camogiers, we grew up, drank, shagged a bit, got ambition – from where? Not school. From TV? From magazines? From looking at our parents and not wanting to be them?

Are cultural shifts contagious?

'Scratch me back, Mary.'

'Have ye fleas, Ollie?'

'I got them off you, ye oul' dog.'

'And you, ye mangy cur?'

Ma scratched Da's back, plunging her nails down his woolly jumper, singing, *'You ain't nothin' but a hound dog!'* The room was scattered with the usual shit – cups of tea gone cold, a spread of the week's tabloids opened at the telly page, a few cans for the match, trainers, camogie slio-tars, a football.

I watched them from the door like a kid might watch a war on the telly. *This is reality,* I was thinking, *but I don't understand it.*

62. Stardust

I can't resist an upturned nose. It's the little touch of snoochiness that the rest of the face just slides into place around. Strictly speaking, a good jaw is a more definite criterion of beauty (bones, darling, bones), but I'll forgive any awkward head if it smiles up in profile, twinkling happily with a nose tip-tilted like a doll, or a Japanese cartoon. It's so damn cute! Turned-down noses look predatory or proud. Straight-across noses look strict and anal. Upturned noses look inquisitive and perky and pleased to see you, and make me crumble inside. I know it's not fair, but there you go. Life and looks just aren't fair.

Decko likes tiny little foetus-features. He's obsessed with getting older and small features age well. Terry likes handsome, older men – sturdy, solid, dependable. Brendan likes faggots. Rock likes nerds and Asians, and nerdy Asians. I like cheeky knackers with behavioural problems, fly black guys, and shy red-headed awkward bastards whom I think I can save from themselves … oh yeah, and obsessing over high-maintenance imaginary relationships that will never come to fruition.

I emailed Decko in work, even though he was in the corporate pig-pen next to mine and it was almost lunch.

From: 'AnthonyBroderick' (RCP14@internalmail.ccp.ie)
To: RCP13@internalmail.ccp.ie
Subject: Target Quotients, Aug

argh!

i hate work!

this is not new but i mean it.

the air-conditioning that recycles diseases,

the headphones that wreck your hair,

the fact that we're not making million s and miming our cowritten tunes on mtv ...

WHY AREN'T WE FAMOUS YET?

i suppose we haven't bloody well earned it ... bah!

what are we afriad of?

why don't we chuck it all in and fuck off tonew york/paris/drug-addicted nirvana?

because:

we are scared of losing the little crappy nothing ness that we have.

which amounts to, well, a job we don't want,

and a contract that isn't working for us.

and a scene that is rapidly shrinking and vapidly boring.

I'M BORED! I'M FED UP! what's the point?!

we are ruled by fear and trapped. discuss.

anto the ranto xxx

p.s. in a shock move, I'm going dairy-free.

it's a;ll your fault, health freak.

i'm sick of being a snot monster -

my poor brain has dried up and shrivelled

thanks to the vast quantities of liquid and mucus

expelled from my nasal cavities.

it's hay-fever and too much cheese.

at first i thought i was allergic to love,

but i've gone khalid-free and that hasn't helped.

From: 'DeclanDunleavey' (RCP13@internalmail.ccp.ie)

To: RCP14@internalmail.ccp.ie

Subject: Received and Registered

why aren't we famous?

cos were broke!

why cant we leave?

cos were broke!

why cant we quit our jobs?

cos were fuckin broke!

at least were tryin ...

and who wants a crappy posh cunt job

when a crappy poor cunt job is easier to walk out of?

the scenes alright ...

its where i met Mully and the best sex ever!! ooh ...

'hes a hottie/kinda spotty/got a great botty' ...

i think ive just wrote a chorus ...

also have seen a flat we might want.

its Brendans old one. remember it?

U shagged Paul in his flatmates bed. haha!

gotta go. bitch face cow breathin down neck.

chill. itll be ok.

get over Kahlid and world will be pretty again.

Art Decko

p.s. haha!

dairy free and the addictive lifestyle options.

next stop – yoga. U will be my yoga bitch!

unless Kahlid ropes U into football ... dont do it ...

think of ur da in the shower. ick!

i reccomend:

'lots of hankies/for the snots/and the wankies/over Kahlid and his mots'

another chorus!

its a good day for the band and our fabulous future.

Every day I tell myself that nothing really matters. I know that we're all just atoms, stardust, and that every collapsed star will fall into the sun long after we're all dead. It's a small comfort to know that bits of me will glimmer in the sky for light years to come, even if there is no conscious matter left to appreciate it. But for now, my conscious self wants the comfort of sushi, and a penthouse apartment, and the adoration of millions, and a cocoon of fame, and sex with Khalid, and sleep with Khalid, and dreams that I'll forget as soon as I wake up in my perfect life. How can anyone be satisfied with what they have, when there's always more to want?

Consciousness sucks.

63. The coefficient of well-being

We moved into Brendan's old apartment that Sunday – it was deadly! We took photos so our ma's could see how swanky it was. I took the blue bedroom cos I'd already shagged Brendan's former flatmate in it. Luckily he'd moved out. We waved Brendan goodbye from our new posh windows that only opened a few centimetres in case you wanted to chuck yourself out of it and spoil the immaculately paved courtyard below.

We had a gate with an intercom, an alarm, tagged trees, softly glowing street lamps along the neat little garden that looked so pretty and unreal from inside, as if it would never grow, or make you sneeze. The overall effect was soothing, as if your neighbours need barely exist. Who wants neighbours anyway? The only signs of life were faintly flickering TVs and computer screens, or the odd glimpse of a hand or foot behind curtains. We found that people moved mostly alone through the courtyard, which was efficient and pleasant enough to carry you to your door with a feeling of well-being, without making you want to linger. It was brilliantly done, like an advert you don't realize you've seen until you've bought the chocolate bar.

NEW APARTMENT CHECKLIST

1. Clothes: go through wardrobe and chuck out all the junk I don't wear anymore. Unless it's from an ex. Or could be used as fancy dress/drag (should times get tough, do not diss the possibility of getting drugged up, dressed up and miming for a living. NB isn't that already my job? Arf!)
2. Hair products: 2 gels, 2 shampoos, conditioner, a range of bleaches and dyes (just in case I get bored in a languid, *nouveau-riche* stylée)
3. Skin-care products: razor + blades, shaving foam, after-shave balm, post-shave moisturizer, exfoliator, cleanser, toner, regular moisturiser, wax (eek!), fake tan, foot scrub
4. New bathroom stuff: towels, face-cloths, hand-towels, shower curtain, rugs (yellow)
5. Posters: Kylie (the official icon of the new apartment), and Brad Pitt (for

the bedroom. Maybe I'm in with a chance now that Jennifer is toast. Hehehe!)

6. Money: deposit and first month's rent = 2 x 575 = 1150 yoyos (eek again!)
7. New key-ring: existing key-ring is sure to be unwieldy. Get a cute one (yellow)
8. New kitchen stuff: cleaning products, own cutlery, dish-cloths, glasses, plates, bowls, mugs (yellow)
9. Bedsheets: Habitat. Not white (or yellow) cos of stains. Think durable and cosy (brushed flannel? possibly in shades of grey)
10. Music: hi-fi and happy, stylish CDs befitting fabulous, upbeat lifestyle (donate moany old Britpop phase to Oxfam)
11. Condoms: both freebies (for the commoners) and bought (if one wants to impress)
12. Booze: any

We drank ourselves silly and had to stash the empty cans under the sink cos we'd forgotten to buy bin-liners and the landlord was coming round the next morning before work to have us sign the lease. Then we fell giggling into our beds in an alcoholic stupor and probably dreamt about all the guys we'd happily shag in the next year, in our new beds, in our swanky apartment, on our way to the top, in our same old brand-new lives.

64. The new rule of acceptable uncool (coupling)

The dawn chorus woke me at 5 a.m.

Beep BEEP Beep! Beep BEEP Beep!
Beep BEEP Beep! Beep BEEP Beep!

> **snogged Alex!**
> **yeah 2 years of**
> **flirting have**
> **paid off**
> **OHMIGOD! we're**
> **officially**
> **TOGETHER!**
> **...hope I didn't**
> **wake u up.N**
> **Options**

I was delighted, even though other people's relationships are so meaning-less – Naomi and Alex had been living a classmate-flirtation that was hit-ting the two-year mark with nary a slip of tongue between them. Cherished moments at the photocopier and tender fragments of conversation snatched over communal coffees had blossomed into picnics on the beach, cham-pagne, roses ... they'd done it all, and now, at last, a result! It was fantas-tic – I'd never have to spend another hour-and-a-half analyzing one of Alex's ambiguous text messages.

No one has demons any more – that's so New Romantic – but we do have imps. The Guilty Conscience imp, the Envy imp, the Naughty-but-Nice imp ... my little Self-Pity imp started whining, *'But what about meee ...?'* The little bastard, he was right!

Whatever happened to the meaningless obsessions and crushes we all used to agonize over? How come Naomi's actually *happened*? It was unheard of in the Rulebook of the Terminally Single. Then I realized that this latest weird twist meant that everyone, *everyone*, was dating – bar me.

Decko and Mully had been going steady for a year – a year of avoiding gay bars, eating ice cream on the sofa, renting videos and having regular sessions of sex and yoga. Rock had Kevin, and assorted international lovelies for some light relief. Terry had 'a work in progress' named Peter, who was older, besuited and married to his work – but still had time for weekend debauchery. Victor had some guy he couldn't shake off no matter how hard he tried – but if he's stuck to your dick, it's more difficult, right? Brendan, who had declared Islam retarded and dangerous and had been dropped by a Muslim friend when he first came out, was now seeing a cute, girlish, lapsed Muslim refugee who shared his atheistic bitching streak.

'If Khalid chooses Allah over the cock, that's just tough on you. He's cute, he's funny, but if he's a fag then he's probably going to be unhappy as long as he's religious. I hope not, but … Move on.'

Much as it suspiciously smacked of Scientology, perhaps I had to forget about Khalid. Despite not seeing him, I thought about him all the time. I guess he was the reason why, as everyone else was cosy-coupling, I'd been the last to modernize.

I stuck on the radio to cover the buzz of thoughts in my head, buried myself in my Habitat brushed-flannel covers in shades of grey, and tried not to let the idea of Khalid keep me awake. But it's hard to sleep with the radio on, and harder to sleep with a hard-on.

65. Ask Anto

It was great having our own place and being responsible for just our own filth. I lived in happy squalor for the first week, rolling home tipsy after work and letting my washing pile up, littering CDs and magazines all over the room, but Decko's queeny perfection soon put me to shame. I had to keep up in the Fabulous Gay Lifestyle game, so I dusted, and tidied, and even tried to like the smell of bleach. After all, the room had served me well for a shag before I moved in, so I had to keep it up to scratch, if only for the sake of sex.

Jen came round for tea, bickies and a gossip about everybody's love-life. She was still with her chap, who was still acting a little bit odd – 'He won't *row* with me, what's wrong?' – though his family just adored her. Girls always infiltrate the family as a way of getting their claws deeper into their man. If they start getting on better with his family then him, the relationship is doomed, but I bit my tongue – Jen doesn't like reality getting in the way of her plans for eternal romance, which is fair enough.

'But, oh, Anto, I'm so worried about Khalid. Have you seen him?'

'Not in a while.'

She looked at me squarely, trying to see what that meant. 'Why not?'

I hesitated. 'He's been … acting weird. I'm just cooling it a little between us.'

Jen sighed. 'That's a relief! *I* think he's being pure weird too, but I didn't want to say anything in case – well, it doesn't matter. Did he *say* anything to you?'

'About what?'

Jen waved her biscuit around, dropping crumbs on our retro-patterned carpet, but I let it go. I sensed some gossip in need of an inventive ear.

'It's nothing definite,' Jen said slowly, 'but he *has* been hanging out with *you* a lot – no offence – and he always did kiss as if – I don't know – it just never felt *right*.'

'In what way?'

'It felt … forced. I know he liked me, but it was like he was *trying* to like me too much, trying to really *impress* me with how much he liked me.'

'That's weird. But is that a bad thing?'

'Nooo ... well, yeah! Why should he have to *try*? Oh Anto, I really think Khalid is *gay*!'

'No,' I said. 'Do you think so?'

Jen nodded and I said, 'Well! I think we need another pot of tea.'

Tea is so civilized, it simply begs discreet character assassination. We munched our way through a packet of Jaffa Cakes and Jen told me Khalid's latest adventure.

'We were in the Buttery the other night, cos our results were out – did I tell you I got a First? Yeah, I'm delighted, I don't know *how* I managed it, they must have felt sorry for me! Anyway, some of the lads were doing shots, Khalid was *wasted* and kept hugging Jasper, it was *embarrassing*, he was sitting on his knee and everything – Jasper? He's just this idiot, he doesn't matter – and then Khalid started smoking, and he *never* smokes, and then he started smoking *two* cigarettes, and then he shoved them up his nose, and someone said, "Khalid, that could only be more disgusting if you shoved them up your *arse*." '

We paused. The mental image was too much.

'He didn't?'

'He *did*. He got his trousers down, then his pants – can you believe he wears those horrible patterned thingies? – then he turned round, bent over, and shoved a lit cigarette up his – oh, it was awful!'

'What would Freud say?'

'He was asked to leave, of course, and then he threw three full pints at the staff and got kicked out.'

'Ouch.'

'I mean, it's not just shoving things up his bum, I'd believe that of any old knacker – no offence – but he's been, oh, *moody*. And he was, I don't know if I should –'

'Go on.'

'He was *boasting* about going to gay bars in London with you, like it was all just a laugh for him, and he was showing off to all the guys cos they thought it was disgusting –'

'Yawn.'

'– and talking about how this big black guy called Jay was coming on to him –'

'That's true.'

'– but he was en*joying* it. You could tell he was really chuffed with himself. He even joined the gay society in Trinity and was showing everyone his membership card and complaining that it wasn't for straight guys too! Anto, can you talk to him?'

'I've tried,' I said. 'He doesn't want to listen. I don't think he's even out to himself.'

'But he's a mess! He's making a fool of himself.'

And me.

'If he comes crawling back, I'll listen,' I said. 'But I'm not going chasing him.'

'Why did you fall out?'

I shrugged and pushed the plate of biscuits towards Jen, hoping I made a convincing victim of Khalid's thwarted lust. I doubt it, though. I was far too glad to hear that other people thought Khalid was confused, even if he was the last one to realize.

I began to think that both Cathy and Khalid would probably try to live the straight life, wonder why it was depressing, have a breakdown and a sexual identity crisis at the age of twenty-eight, surprise no one by coming out messily, and hit their thirties with unresolved teenage angst and a lot of debauched catching up to do.

Then Decko came back and we had a good bitch about the bitches in work instead.

66. Pride

We joined the march late cos we were still hungover from the night before. By the time we reached Trinity the queers were turning into College Green, so we hopped in the middle of the whistle-blowers, bad drag and rainbow banners, pretending we were bright-eyed and politicized enough to have been there all along. I think we were between the Aids Alliance and the Bi-Irish gang. How great would it be to be bi? You could piss even more people off.

The amount of bad drag! I was totally fucking proud of how well Mr McGinnity ('Call me Aunt Fanny!') looked compared to the teenage munchkins in their sisters' mascara and tights. He was a real diva! I was right about the yellow – there's just not enough yellow in the world. He was there with the missus, who was nearly the most manly creature in amongst the Butterfly Club – trannies of all sorts, being way too glam and getting wolf-whistles from the crowd – who threw armfuls of kisses right back! There were masses of Dublin jerseys heading in the opposite direction towards Croke Park, and they were bemused but smiling and eventually cheering too – it might have been half taking the piss, but it was cool. I even spotted Cathal amongst them, scratching his head and looking shamefaced, which couldn't be a bad thing. I waved and he pretended not to see me.

It's always a jolt to see so many lesbians out for a change. Then there was Rob and Lenny, two guys I'd been to school with, lurking on the sidelines grinning and holding hands – I hadn't seen those two out before, that was a surprise. It was a proper day out because Ivana Bacik was there, dancing off her tits again – go the woman! She got my vote for sheer bloody stamina.

Decko and Mully held hands. Rock waved to Kevin, who was watching from Dublin Castle – he's too closeted and paranoid to march – but that was OK, cos Rock got to scope the talent with me.

'They have a Queer Muslim gang at London Pride,' I said wistfully.

'Yeah, well, he ain't there either,' said Rock. 'Ooh, look at him – he's just your type!'

'Who, him? He's the guy who gave you crabs last Paddy's Day.'

'Fuck, is that who it was? Well, I wasn't blind drunk, he's a cutie!'

Terry had brought a picnic for the Party in the Park at Christchurch.

'Sweetie, I've got two of the major food groups – beer and chocolate. Help yourself!'

'Let the bitching commence!'

The best bit about the party is that it's free and open to all, so you always get the smackheads mulling around between chaps in leather with their arses hanging out, home-made drag queens, and born-again lesbians. There were a few stolid gardaí, a bouncy castle for the kids, Owen's drug-dealer (he wasn't wearing his Burberry cap, which meant he was off-duty), some young lads in tracksuits hanging round the outskirts as if they were there by accident (Terry thought they were rent), and lots of really cute guys'n'dolls just cruising. Yeah!

The boybands were officially 'Not as good as us!' so we were even more mad jealous cos we weren't performing.

'Would Daniel have done it?'

'Yeah, course he would.'

'Will we see him here next year?'

'Maybe ...'

'We'll have to haul him out!'

'Deal!'

Me and Decko and Mully nipped off for a takeaway breakfast during the thank-you speeches, and nipped back again to buy tickets for the club that night. We talked to everyone we knew for about two seconds each – 'Howaya luv?' 'Happy Pride!' – and zombie-walked home to get a few hours kip before the real party began.

The club started off brilliant, three floors of sweaty men looking for their hole. I sank a few drinks and did the hoor tour. After a couple of hours of the same faces – of which mine was one, of course – I began to get ... bored of it all. Poppers, drink, exes ... it wasn't that the men weren't up for it, or sexy. It wasn't that the music wasn't hard and happy and hypnotic. It wasn't that I wasn't proud to be part of it ...

I tried to tell Decko, to a backdrop of go-go dancers, arse-pinching queens, perky nipples, backslapping, glances, beefy arms raised to the thump of the music and the stuttering lights –

'Have another drink,' Decko said soothingly.

'I'll have a water,' I said.

Bam.

It hit me.

Truth was, I'd heard of Gay Fatigue before. I just never thought it would happen to me.

I'd overdosed on the sheer glamour of being a fabulous fag.

I was all fagged out.

I needed a break from the scene. I needed nights on the sofa with a proper dinner and a video, a cuddle instead of wild, abandoned, random sex.

Mully had had twelve vodkas and Decko was propping him up, although he could barely stand himself. It was so sweet!

I closed my eyes to the disco tits, the glitter, the kissy lips and the heave of bodies. I took a deep breath and admitted the truth.

It was high time that Anto Broderick got a proper fucking boyfriend.

There. I said it. I'm needy. Gay pride!

67. capitalist_kid@gaydar.co.uk

Capitalist Kid (20 years old)
Area Ireland – Dublin
City Dublin, Ireland
Viewed 521 times

GENERAL INFORMATION
I am a Single Gay Man.
Interested in meeting Single Man
For Relationship, Friendship, 1-on-1 Sex
Between 18 & 24 years old

ABOUT
Typical fag, into pop and all that rubbish, likes a beer and a smoke and a movie and, yeah, a shag is good too. The end!

LOOKING FOR
I'm into beautiful losers, arty idiots and atheistic bitches.

TYPES I LIKE
Clubbers, Footballers, Geeks, Preppies, Short Guys, Tall Guys, Twinks

LEISURE ACTIVITIES
Cinema/Movies, Clubbing, Entertaining, Music

PERSONAL INFORMATION
Occupation Dancer
Height 5'8" (173 cm)
Body Type Slim
Ethnic Origin Caucasian
Hair Colour Blond
Eye Colour Blue
Attire Trendy
Out Yes
Dick Size Average

Cut/Uncut Uncut
Body Hair Some
Orientation Gay
Role Versatile
Practise Safer Sex Always
Smoke Yes
Drink Socially
Drugs Socially

HOBBIES & FAVOURITE THINGS
Food Junkfood
Music Kylie, Madonna, R&B – popular trash!
Author Why read when you can see it on TV ...
Film Moulin Rouge
Actor Brad Pitt
Actress Nicole Kidman
TV Show CD:UK
Holiday Destination Spain (for the sun and cheap beer)
City London (for the clubs)
Country America (for the dollars)
Club Popstarz, GAY, Heaven
Bar/Pub The Front Lounge

68. Chemistry

It was like breaking up with someone, even though we'd never swapped bodily fluids. When summer showers fell against window panes, I thought about him. I found myself drinking my coffee milky with three sugars, just like he did. I thought I saw strangers in the street wearing his face, and every conversation ended with, 'Oh yeah, Khalid used to –' before me and whoever would roll our eyes and change the subject abruptly.

I was living in a really soppy ballad.

Of course, putting myself up for grabs on Gaydar was simply swapping one gay lifestyle option for another, but it passed the time. In one sweeping fortnight I'd exchanged photos with a few guys (no nude shots, thanks!), flirted online, and met some of them for a beer or whatever. It was kind of exciting at first, but everyone was either an ex of someone I knew, or a guy I recognized from a shop where he used to work, or slutty, or boring, or had been blatantly lying about who they were. 'Damon' from Tallaght turned out to be Debbie – 'I love my gay friends and one of these days, I'm gonna convert one of you!' I took her pint right out of her hand, skulled it, and walked much too calmly out of the pub. But basically, I found that computer dating lacked chemistry.

I was mentally debating how to kindly dump one specimen of minger-hood whom I'd stupidly agreed to meet even though I didn't fancy him – my Self-Delusion imp was telling me, *Oh, but he's such a laugh!* – when I knocked someone's elbow at the bar. His pint imploded on the floor, splashing his old-skool Adidas trainers.

'I'm sorry, shit, I'm sorry – what are you drinking? I'll get you an –'

'It's OK,' he said.

My eyes flew upwards to his *really cute* face.

'You wanna share an E instead?' he said.

I grinned. This was it. *Chemistry.*

69. Sixty-nine

Oh man, there's nothing like a sweaty sixty-nine! Gobbing a good juicy cock and being slurped on upside down, pumping away at both ends like a great big double-headed dildo – it's fucking magic!

70. Kitsch bitch

I realized that how I experienced life had changed without Khalid. Time seemed to go much faster, more things seemed to happen, and yet there was nothing to measure this passing of time against. The centre of my universe, the reason I got up in the morning, the screw that my life turned on had been knocked askew.

When Khalid came round at 3 a.m. after phoning me drunk and asking to talk, I watched him speak and took very little of it in.

He tripped over his own words, as if reciting a rehearsed but hurried monologue. He fidgeted, he played with his hands, his eyes flew round the room, settling for a second here or there – the leather couches, the prints on the wall, the breakfast bar – but he didn't really see it. Our room was just the backdrop to his personal drama. I could understand that, but I couldn't understand what the hell he wanted. Not after all this time. I remember bits of his speech, bits that seemed relevant to what he was talking around, rather than really saying.

'I'm too old to be a virgin.'

'I like her, but – how do I know, man?'

'She wants to sleep with me, but I'm not sure. I sort of want to, but … first time, I couldn't get it up!'

'Do you fancy her?' I asked abruptly, snapping out of the dwam, the light diffusing through the curtains like smoke, Khalid blurring round the edges.

'She's a beautiful girl,' Khalid said.

'So fuck her,' I said.

Khalid shifted on his couch. Stared at the floor. Stared up.

'Yeah,' he said. Then, like he'd just remembered himself, he said, 'So! What about you? How's the love-life? Seeing anyone?'

'Yeah, I've got a fella.'

'Wh – have you?'

'Mm.'

'Wow – is he – where'd you meet?'

'Oh, in a bar. Drugs, sex, relationship. You know.'

'That's, *wow*, that's – cool. Is he cute?'

'He's real cute.'

'What's his name?'

'Chris. Look, Khalid, it's late – do you want a cup of tea? Or a drink?'

'No, I'm good.'

'Well then …'

He was still a little drunk. It took a moment. 'Do you want me to go?' he asked quietly.

'I suppose you better. It's late.'

He shuffled in his seat. I would normally have asked him to stay, and he would normally have refused. 'Are you meeting Chris tomorrow?'

'I'm going to *work*, Khalid. But I'm meeting Chris after work.'

'OK. Cool. Well.' He stood up uncertainly, and I smiled.

'See ya around sometime.'

'Yeah, give me a ring,' Khalid said.

'Sure,' I said.

I knew I would – but not just yet.

He left. I drew back the curtains, opened the windows as far as they would open, and lit a cigarette. I blew smoke rings into the black and orange night, my nose pressed against the window frame. The smoke-rings sighed, quivered, and were gone.

I am fascinated by the quality of light. Street lamps. The sky. A soft bulb glowing from the centre of a room. I love to feel the quality of air, to imagine slipping unconscious through the particles of light, sublimating into something less tangible than dust. Wouldn't you love to be lighter than air?

The solidity of everyday life disturbs me sometimes. The earthy reality of birth and death and indoor plumbing. The glassy bars full of people, drinking. The oblivion of everyone to their own insect existence. Even watching other people eat makes me queasy – to enjoy it so much, to smack your lips and rub your belly and gloat over food – it's like public masturbation.

I wish everything was as kitsch as a cuckoo clock. I'd love to be that little wooden bird, programmed to chirrup happily on the hour, every hour, for all time.

71. Lunatic, Frounge

I was in the Frounge with Chris when this random crazy guy came and sat at our table. I tried to ignore him but he just sat there uninvited, staring at us, back and forth across our conversation. Chris, who was a bit of a cool bastard, turned to him and said, 'What?' We would totally have ignored him except he was young and quite good-looking.

Crazy guy launched into an eager, rambling speech about the media, and truth, and all this psycho-babble that really said, 'Hey folks, I've forgotten to take my medication today!'

By the end, he was like, 'Guys, I don't know about you, but do you ever get the feeling that corporate powers are lying to us?'

'Isn't that their job?' I asked.

He looked blank. He continued. 'With, I don't know, adverts and promotions and media and television and government funding, how do we know what's real?'

'If you can buy it, it's real,' I said. He looked scandalized.

'No! See, what I mean is, everything is lies and perpetuated by Capitalism –'

Bla, bla, bla.

I noticed a guy from the Arabic fast-food joint across the road come in and whisper to one of the bartenders. He pointed at our loony friend. Chris was talking to him as if he was a kid, looking at his notebook – 'I'm collecting people's words, people's stories, people's *truths*' – and scribbled something in it as the bartender came over and tapped Crazy Guy on the shoulder. He jolted.

'This guy a friend of yours?'

'I know these people!' Crazy Guy yelled. 'I'm just talking! You're part of the conspiracy, man! You're a liar, you're lying to everyone here –'

'Come on sir, time to leave.'

It took both the bouncers to throw Crazy Guy and his Notebook of Wisdom out on his ass. We went back to our pints, shrugging, smiling and rolling our eyes to an imaginary heaven at the people round the table beside us.

'What did you write in his notebook?'

'I wrote, *You are a paranoid schizophrenic and you need medical help. If it really bothers you that people lie, go lock yourself alone in a box.*'

'Nice one, haha!'

I made a mental note to exaggerate the story for Khalid's benefit. Then we changed the subject back to ourselves.

72. Textual intercourse

'I've been getting these calls from one of my photographers,' Cathy said.

'Well, good. More work?'

'Not really, it's more … personal.'

I knew exactly where this was going, but I kept my voice flat and my eyes on my perfect latte. It was expertly done with a milk float on the strong, dark coffee beneath, topped with a frothy head of whisked milk and a light sprinkling of chocolate dust. It seemed too beautiful to drink.

'She took an interest after this photoshoot we did in Ballymun, which was an experience – they're more *normal* than you'd expect, the locals I mean, though I suppose *you'd* know that more than I would – anyway, she asked me for my number because she thought I'd done a *marvellous* job when I had to hang off the back of this tractor-and-trailer thing. I had to wear a shawl, it was horrible! My nose is all pink in the final shots. I'm sure they airbrushed it in to make me look more like a peasant! But she's been texting me, and it's not about work – in fact, she wants to know do I want to go for a drink?'

'She just asked you? Straight out?'

'She's more out than straight, if you know what I mean.' (I cringed.) 'But, well, no, we've been texting each other for a while, I don't know *why*, she just sends me odd little messages, and when I reply, it seems to go on for hours!'

'So don't reply.'

'But I *like* her!' Cathy said with big eyes. 'She's very pretty, for a lesbian. Do you think I'd be leading her on?' she asked demurely, lapping at her cappuccino.

'I don't know. What have you said to her?'

'Oh, nothing,' Cathy said vaguely. 'This and that. We talk about, oh, rugby and where to buy nice flat shoes and our favourite Bath Bombs and that sort of thing. And guess what – I couldn't meet her because I was in the pub already – with your mum! She'd been watching our rugby match – we lost, it was *hilarious* – with a pal of hers from camogie, not that there's much of a G.A.A. crossover, but we had a good laugh over the old white wines. You never told me your mum was so cool!'

'Cool? She's still into the Spice Girls and watches Buffy, for Christ's sake!'

'All very Girl Power,' Cathy mused. 'If I didn't know any better, I'd say that's why you're gay! Why are you still staring at your coffee? Aren't you going to drink it?'

I held it up. 'It's so perfect. It looks like me and Khalid would in bed.'

'You mean you're on top? *Really*? Gosh. It's funny, but that's what me and your mum had the best laugh about – you and your men!'

'What? You talked about what me and *Kha* – I mean, what me and *Chris* do in bed?'

'Oh, don't be silly,' Cathy said. 'We all know you and Khalid are never going to happen, and Chris is just to get over him. No, we were laughing about how you and Decko are bound to get together eventually. You know, when you're both thirty and Decko realizes that looks aren't everything.'

I spluttered on my latte, splattering the table with mine and Khalid's creamy hot spunk.

Cathy chattered on, oblivious.

'You know, I think your mum might be good for me. Married. No hidden agenda.'

'It must be tough being irresistable,' I retorted. 'Just keep your dykey paws off my mum. She'd probably bloody like it too much!'

73. Joyriders

Every time I went home I wondered *why*? In the door, cup of tea, boom! Instant boredom. No one ever changed. No one ever did anything new. In fairness, neither did I, but at least I was off my tits every night of the week, trying to make exciting things happen. I had plans, you know?

```
abc           336/1
Yawn. YAWN.
YAAAAAWN!!!
'You have now
reached Planet
Home. Please
postpone your
actual life for
the duration of
your stay.'
        Options
```

'Emily's found a new man,' Ma said, as I tried for the umpteenth time to retune the VCR. 'He's a Garda.'

'She's sleeping with the enemy!' I yelled, louder than I meant to.

'She is *not* sleeping with him,' Ma said, a firm believer that telling a lie loud enough made it true.

'This video is never going to work.'

'Jenny's in Belfast with the man.'

'That's Da's fault for buying it off the back of a lorry.'

'Zak's on that computer, *too* long.'

'Where *is* Da till I tell him what a piece of crap this is?'

'At the match.'

It was always *the* match, as if I was supposed to know which one.

'Have a tea-cake,' Ma said.

'Those aren't bloody tea-cakes, they're marshmallow … *yokes*.'

'Well, we always used to call them tea-cakes,' Ma said. 'Look, it says it on the box. Used to get them for sixpence.'

'Ma, it's the noughties. Wake up and smell the euro. Jesus, this place reeks of *damp*. I never noticed before.'

'No, *you* wouldn't, with your head in the clouds and up to your ears in hair-gel and scent. It's not like I don't clean the place, you know. The council's been promising to fix it for years, *years*, and they never once –'

Yadda, yadda.

'Yeah, you're right,' I said. 'So! I hear you met Cathy at one of her rugby matches. What's she like, her and her rugby?'

'She's a tight gesha,' Ma said, picking up a magazine and wiping her fingers on it. 'But those lovely legs are so easily bruised! I told her to stick with the modelling – she's so *glamorous*,' Ma said, flicking through the flimsy mag. It flashed in primary colours, diets, tits, celebrity faces –

'Now you know why we think she's a big dyke.'

'Anto, don't say that. You of all people!'

'Oh, don't be daft. She's as gay as, as gay as – she's as gay as *I* am.'

'Well not everyone can be as out as you. Give the poor girl a chance to defend herself.'

'It's not a crime any more, Ma,' I said, exasperatedly. 'And how *is* that magazine supposed to help you become a radical feminist, exactly?'

'We have to keep up to date with how celebrity culture perpetuates traditional gender roles in the male gaze of the camera and its subsequent portrayal of unrealistic ideals of femininity,' Ma sniffed.

'And you think Cathy should stick to the modelling?'

'But she's *lovely*,' Ma said. 'I mean, *look* at that one from Destiny's Child, they were *never* as real as the Spice Girls. The Spice Girls had wobbly bits and were so *needy*. You just *knew* they'd all be looking for nice boyfriends after they made their money.'

'Is that good?'

'Of course it's good! I've a good mind to take your Cathy under my wing. At least until she realizes what she's worth and finds herself a good man.'

'Eh, right, Ma.'

Zak is so responsible he even rations his time on computer games in case he gets addicted. I found him clearing out his wardrobe.

'I ended up dreaming in SimCity. It was getting out of hand. Is this top too gay?'

'Yeah. I'll take it.'

'Here you go. I'd need a really fit girlfriend to get away with it!'

I tried it on.

'Cathal's gonna love me in this!'

'Cathal Woods?'

'Yeah, he's such a fag.'

'He's a *psycho*,' Zak said. 'Da kicked him off the team for bein' an alco, and now he's drivin' cars into walls and burnin' them out, he's *nuts*.'

'He's a loser,' I said – but of course, that only made him seem more attractive, then. 'Thanks for the top! I'll wear it for me new fella.'

'I hope he's a better catch than Cathal Woods.'

'Sure he's only gorgeous! And the *size* of his –'

'I don't want to know!'

'– wallet.'

'Hey! Tell me more! Is he loaded?'

I ate as much free food as I could find, air-kissed the folks goodbye, and skipped off back to the bleached, aspirational blandness of my new apartment. As I crossed the yard, Mr McGinnity came skittering out of his flat, waving theatrically.

'Jesus! Howaya, Mr McGinnity, what's up? I saw you at Pride –'

'Yes, yes, thanks, but – Anto, did you hear about the car, did your mother say?'

'Say what?'

Mr McGinnity was agitated, breathless, and kept glancing round furtively, as if we were comedy spies in a black-and-white movie.

'No, no, she mightn't ... it's nothing, it's just, it's *Cathal Woods*, he ...'

'What about him?'

'Look, come inside for a cup of tea, and –'

'No, eh, I really have to go, I've a date with Chris, that's my –'

'Ssshhh! Oh, Anto, *look*. I have to tell you this and you're *not* going to like it, but that little *blackguard*', coming from Mr McGinnity, this sounded damning, '*Cathal Woods* has been telling stories about you – right or wrong, I don't know – but he's in a right state –'

'I could tell you a couple of stories about *him*,' I said sharply.

Mr McGinnity, hunched in his tweed coat, empty black-eyed windows staring down at us, put a finger to his lips. 'I wouldn't, if I were you.'

'This is ridiculous,' I said. 'What's Cathal supposed to have said? What's he *done*?'

'He's been saying that you, eh, made advances towards him,' Mr McGinnity said, shaking his head. An old dog trailed by, a three-time amputee baby doll in its mouth. Litter rustled, and Mr McGinnity clawed his jacket tighter round him. 'And last week, he spray-painted "Anto Broderick is a faggot" on a car and burnt it out. So watch your back.'

'He should watch his,' I said grimly, 'or he might just get what he really wants!'

'Just be careful, Anto.'

I forced a laugh. 'Don't worry about me, Mr McG!'

I stopped myself breaking into a sweat – or into a run – by counting ads for the revamped School Disco club night all the way home. There were seventeen. None of them advertised the fucking retards you had been to school with.

74. Kinky Irish cream

Khalid invited me and Jen over for dinner. 'We haven't all hung out for too long, man. No significant others, just us.' I met Jen outside his block.

'He probably wants to decide who he fancies more,' I said.

'He made such a big deal about not cooking pig!' Jen grumbled. 'He says the smell of *pig flesh* cooking is just like the smell of burning humans. How would he know? Cos he read it in the bloody Koran?'

'Hello!' Khalid called from a window. 'The door should open but the intercom's busted! Come on up!'

Jen looked mortified. 'Did he hear me?'

'Probably. So what?'

I'm in the lead! I thought smugly.

Dinner was passable – not bachelor chow, but no evidence of gay flair either – but his apartment, now that I saw it sober, was gorgeous. Pastel colours, bold, simple furniture, bright prints on every wall.

'Congrats on the apartment! It's fabulous.'

'You've seen more of it than Jen! Come on Jen, I'll show you the bedroom.' Jen looked at me quizzically, but I feigned nonchalance and went to play with the stereo.

The Bang and Olufsen sound system said *Gay!* but the Maroon 5 CD in it said *Straight!* No wonder the poor guy was confused – he was trying to live two cultures at once.

What really summed it up was when he talked about David Beckham. He admired him as a footballer, yeah, but spent more time banging on about his hair.

'I really admire Beckham,' he said, going dreamy about the eyes. 'He's not afraid to let men fancy him. Man, he's such a style guru! Everybody wants a bit of him.'

'He's too womany,' Jen said.

'I thought you liked guys who looked like their mums!' Khalid said. 'I thought you liked my feminine side! We used to do the dishes together, that was nice.'

'Well, I'm not doing them tonight, if that's what you're hinting!'

'I'll do them,' I said.

'Nah, it's fine –'

'It's OK, I will. I'm making tea anyway.'

'You know who's really girlie in our class?' Jen mused. 'Damien Walsh.'

'Who's he?'

'The one with the ears.'

'The cute one?'

'Eh, yeah, he is cute, but he's feminine. Though he tries to hide it by being overly polite.'

'I see him everywhere. We're always in the gym at the same time, but he never says hello. I wasn't sure who he was at first. And he's in my Ballroom Dancing class.'

'I didn't know you did Ballroom Dancing!'

'Oh, I'm not much good. Damien's way better! It's a bit like football, though ...'

I came in with the tea, and Jen broke Khalid off mid-sentence, to throw some gossip at me.

'Oh! Do you know who I saw the other day and I meant to say – *Dave*!'

'Which Dave? My Dave?'

'Yeah. Anto, he looks *awful*. He looks *ill*. Is he on something?'

'Like what?'

'Drugs. He looks *seriously* ill.'

'He's probably stressed. Exam time.'

'Exams are over.'

'He's doing his Masters.'

'Well, *I* don't know, but I hope he's got checked out recently.'

'Jen, your concern for his health is touching,' I said in a sing-song Australian-soap accent, 'but it's none of your damn business!'

'He could have Aids,' Jen sniffed, in a very Ma-like way.

'I'm sure he doesn't.'

'Are you sure?'

'He's been checked out, not that I should even be telling you. He's not bloody ill at all, you're imagining it.'

'You never know. I hope you got checked out after being with him!'

'Darling, Dave got the all-clear. And I can assure you that anything I had, Dave would have caught!'

'So you're having unsafe sex then …'

'You never know whose bed you'll fall into next!' Khalid said with a laugh. 'You end up with all sorts, never mind those saunas. Man, what are they like?'

'I wouldn't know,' I said, 'they're more for the *closet cases*.'

Khalid laughed some more. 'You'll have to let me read that Coming-Out Guide you promised me!'

Jen looked shocked for a second, then gave me a delighted thumbs-up and a wink while Khalid poured the milk.

'No probs,' I said. 'You can even show it to Damien Walsh in the locker room.'

'Yeah. But you were meant to be my gym-buddy this year!'

'I guess Chris works me out too good.'

'Man, tell us more!'

I was *so* winning this round.

'Well, I've brought a bottle of Bailey's. We could do shots in honour of a good blow-job!'

75. Anto's guide to coming out (for Khalid)

(As in telling folks you're a big queer, kiddo.)

The first step is crucial – coming out to **yourself**.

Say it.

'I am gay.'

See?!?

That wasn't so bad!

Or was it?

Bad News (Boo!)

Well, most of us have had **issues** about our sexuality. It happens cos of those currently unavoidable years of homophobic horseshit force-fed to us from just about everywhere, from a very young age, from the playground to the TV.

Good News (Yay!)

The best antidote to stupid homophobia is going out and experiencing the highs, lows and sheer normality of our gay lives. It's called **reality**, cos **being gay** is exactly like **being straight** but with more **style**.

So now you're coming out – **what took you so long?**

Here are some reasons people **don't** come out:

1. Fear
2. Uncertainty
3. Inexperience
4. Straight Life™

Fear, mostly of other people's reactions. My own personal reaction to homophobic abuse is **'Who gives a fuck?'**, but not everyone is as **cool** as me.

Homophobia does exist and most of us have to deal with it. People will make ignorant and hurtful remarks from time to time – often without even realizing it. The biggest challenge of being lesbian, gay or bisexual is rising above the idiocy of people who won't accept you for yourself. It won't always be easy, but it's easier just knowing that there are other people, friends and acquaintances who face the same problems all the time – **gay friends, a youth group, drinking mates on the scene** – all essential accessories to overcoming negativity!

In the meantime, you should practise your **'Fuck you!' attitude** in your own time, until you get as good at it as I am.

Uncertainty, whereby people wonder if their gay urges are **'a phase'**. The short answer is **no**. If you have sexual feelings for people of the same sex, you're gay. Your sexuality will not change much over time, though if you're bi, you might go through boy/girl phases of attraction. So stop thinking that just cos you hate Kylie and like football you might just be straight after all!

A lot of people who haven't yet seen the glory of their gay potential think that if they ignore their gay feelings, the feelings will go away. **They won't**. It is true that sexuality may be more **fluid** than the simple **gay/straight/bi** guidelines we like to stick with, but you'll probably identify **strongly** with one of these labels.

Some folk prefer the **Kinsey Scale Test,** where your sexuality falls on a scale of 1-10, 1 being 'perfectly straight' (no gay feelings) and 10 being 'perfectly gay' (no straight feelings).

Where do **you** stand? I'm an 8 or 9, I think, so gay is good enough for me!

Inexperience, or **'How do I know I'm gay if I haven't tried it?'** It's more difficult to try experimental gay snogs, as opposed to experimental straight fumblings, when you're a teenager, cos chances are the only places to go are straight (unless you were a lucky little boy scout or boarding-school inmate). So it figures that you'll probably have tried the straight thing, but the gay thing would mean head-first, full-on gate-crashing a big, scary, queer nightclub (far enough away from home that no one you know will see you going in). **Fact**: the average age that gay males lose their gay virginity is **twenty**. So compared to breeding thirteen-year-olds, we get a late sexual start in life (but ain't it fun trying to catch up?).

If you haven't had a gay experience, you'll know you're gay because you want one (or many). The first experience might be awful – that kinda happens when Dutch courage dictates five pints, a couple of vodkas and a tequila slammer – but if so, don't let that put you off. **It's all part of the journey, baby**. Thanks to our shit-scared schools, your sex education is more likely to be stacks of **porn movies** and lots of **false starts** before you are fully proficient in the joys of gay sex. **Grrr!**

Straight Life™, aka **faking heterosexuality**. This stems from the perception that the straight life is easier.

Newsflash: not if you're gay it ain't. It may be common, it may be expected, it may be the done thing, but if it ain't for you, it won't make you happy.

Most gay people have had straight experiences. Some think coming out is too difficult compared to at least attempting **Straight Life**™. Some enjoy their hetero flings, some don't, most agree that their heart wasn't in it.

Don't believe the hype that Straight Life™ **= love and fulfilment whereas Gay Life = sex and disappointment!**

At its worst, trying to be straight will leave you frustrated, disappointed and missing out on the chance for a truly loving sexual relationship.

Newsflash extra: you can't be happy unless you're honest with yourself about what you want from life. If that includes a **same-sex lover** – great! **Go for it!**

OK, cool. You know you're gay and now you want to do something about it. You want sex, you want love, you want to be comfortable with who you are – and you want others to be comfortable with your sexuality too. In fact, you deserve it. And that means you will have to **come out.** Our society presupposes heterosexuality. If you're gay, at some stage you'll have to acknowledge it. You already have, by telling yourself. **Well done you!**

So what do you do when you want to tell other people?

Coming out is a process. You'll tell different people or groups of people at different stages. Remember that you don't have to tell **anyone** if you **don't want to**. You might be cool with some people knowing you're gay and not others. There are homophobes in the world and no one can blame you for avoiding awkward or dangerous situations. But remember that a) some people will take the news of you're being gay better than you ever expected, and b) the best way to combat prejudices is often to face them head-on. But you don't have to be out to everyone.

It's your choice.

Our lives tend to divide into friends, family and work. These are broadly the three groups you might want to come out to.

Most of us first come out to our closest trusted **friends** whom we are pretty sure will be cool with us being gay. They might be out, or have gay friends, or just have shown a tolerant attitude in the past. Trust me, **most**, but definitely not **all**, friends will have wondered if you are gay. You may or may not have tried to hide it, but anyone's sexuality is a powerful aspect of their lives and bound to make itself known in one way or another. Depending on how clued-in your friends are, they'll probably have noticed.

Your closest friends will be supportive, and probably curious. Be prepared for questions such as, **'How long have you known?'** (**'Forever'**) and **'Who do you fancy?'** (**'Not you, mate'**). If they do take the news badly, give them time to come to terms with it. If they are a good friend, they'll be grateful for your honesty and will probably come with you to clubs before long (and we all need good drinking buddies!).

Friends who aren't so close may be more wary of talking to you directly about your sexuality. They might be worried about looking nosy, or just saying the wrong thing. If they do ask any questions, the best advice is to be **honest** and show them that you're cool talking about being gay. It's an opportunity to do your bit for **gay liberation**. It's good to talk!

Family: Your siblings will most likely react in a similar way to your friends when you tell them you're gay. As they've probably known you longer and more intimately, they are unlikely to be shell-shocked (though it does happen), and sometimes they are more **worried** for you. **Reassure** them!

It's often most difficult to come out to your parents. They are, of course, of an older generation and are often clueless about the realities of modern gay lives. Unfortunately, it ain't all **sex, drugs and disco-dancing**. Their own issues may be **religious, health-conscious, work-related**, or even just worrying about **what the neighbours will say**. Whatever the most dire consequences could be, they'll have thought of it – it's their job. You'll know yourself what they'll be most worried about – prepare some soothing answers. In case it does get out of hand, it's a good idea to **phone a friend** if there's any major problems. If your parents love you (**they do**) then that will be unconditional. They may need a **gay education** – check out the national helpline for parents of gay kids.

It's normal to worry that your folks will be disappointed, angry or tearful. Remember that it's probably a situation they've already imagined and it's partly **your responsibility** to help them understand your sexuality, and gay lives more generally. As for your wider family, it depends how close you are to them if you tell them personally or not. Either way, with both friends and family, your coming out will be news – be prepared for CONGRATULATIONS (or knowing smiles) all round.

Work can be a tricky place to be out. For a start, you probably don't consider your workmates to be close friends, but you do have to interact with them all week. On one hand, it's annoying to have to lie about 'the girlfriend' if it's a bloke you're snuggling up with. But then, you might be concerned about job security, promotion or just slagging if you are out. Some of it depends on **office politics** or how **gender-traditional** your workplace is – like, if you're in the army, probably best to stay in that closet. Anyway, if you would be more comfortable being out at work, then it's probably best to say it casually the next time someone asks about 'the girlfriend' (**'Oh, he's fine ...'**). Take a delight in watching jaws drop, and don't be surprised if all the girls want to hang out with their bestest new gay buddy. And won't the boys be jealous!

It's worth checking out national/work policy on discrimination on the grounds of sexual orientation. If you do work in a homophobic environment (e.g. sports, health professional) then you're faced with the dilemma of either striking a blow for equality by leading with the example of your own happy out existence, or toeing the line and putting up with the shit for the sake of an easy life. OK, I'd rather be out – but I know it's easier said than done.

So think about it!

Good luck!

COMMON COMING-OUT CRISES

Camp: You know, effeminate, limp-wristed, tight T-shirted and good hair kinda guys. In short, the clichéd image of gay men.

A lot of gay guys are concerned about their masculinity. In so many personal ads, for example, they describe themselves as 'straight acting'. Current thinking is – who gives a fuck? Some gay guys are camp and some aren't. Don't beat yourself up over **'seeming gay'**, as if expressing gayness is a weakness. **It isn't**. You do not have to be butch, nor do you have to be camp. **Be yourself, maaan!**

Partying hard: Now that you're out, the temptation is to go **mad** on the scene. Happens all the time! The new freedom you feel can mean an over-indulgence in drink, or drugs, or sex, or really crappy music by third-rate girlbands. **And why not?** So long as you practise safe sex and know your limits, **celebrating** coming out is cool. But don't throw yourself into **party hard** mode as compensation for any **unresolved issues** about your sexuality. If you need to talk things through, then your mates should be there for you. Or go to the pros and try a gay helpline. Then you can get back to **partying hard and healthy**!

Love vs. Sex: Fact of life, guys are horny. It may seem easy at first to live the slapper life that guys excel at, but you probably feel that, beyond the sex, you really want love. **Aw! That's so sweet ...** so while you might fall in and out of bed with a few guys, you'll have an eye out for **The One**, and that's cool. **Golden rule** – don't mess people round. One-night stands are fine if that's what you both want – but don't lead people on that there could be more to it if you don't think there is. Then again, it's OK to try dating for a while, to see if it suits you both.

It's **not OK** to keep people hanging on just in case you might want to shag them again. You **can** have a healthy relationship just based on sex (**fuck buddies**) but it usually gets messy when one guy wants something more than just sex. And if you find **love**, then you have to **give in** to it.

True!

76. Double whopper meal deal

'I read your style guide – you can have it back!'

'But it's for you.'

'You don't expect me to follow it?'

'Of course I do!'

Rock scoffed his chicken-wings with gusto. Flecks of barbecue sauce bloodied up his stubble.

'But Anto,' he said (through mouthfuls of chicken flesh), 'I don't *want* to look the same as everyone else.'

'Well you *should*,' I said. 'How else are you supposed to get all the normal, decent guys?'

'Oh, normal and decent, what rubbish! All the normal and decent guys are *boring*. You don't fancy normal and decent guys, so I don't know why you'd want to *dress* like one. You should go buy a tracksuit and cruise the Phoenix Park, that's where all the love-hungry fucked-up knackers are!'

Unfortunately, he may have had a point.

'How's Kevin?' I asked, just to change the subject.

'Oblivious to my infidelity, which is how it should be. I, however, am *not* oblivious to *his*!' Rock declared, waving a chicken-wing around. 'I found his profile on a gay Asian website, which I was cruising myself, of course. They love my blond floppy hair!'

'It's a niche market, I suppose.' I slurped my milkshake and eyed all the guys sliding by the window. Baseball caps are so snoochy …

'I have some bad news for you.'

'Not your da?'

'Eh? Oh, him. Nah, he's fine, but I'd have my brother *certified* if I could. No, it's about your Chris.'

'What about him?'

'I saw him in The Boilerhouse last night. He looks really good naked but he's not too fussy about where he hides the sausage!'

'You're kidding.'

'Nope, sorry.' Rock started on his cheesy chips, strings of liquefying yellow stretching from the bowl to his happily munching mouth. He smacked his lips. 'Yum! He begged me not to tell you, and he *was* hammered, but I thought you should know that your boyfriend's a bit of a dirty bird. Like me!'

'That's the end of Chris,' I said, stealing some of Rock's cheesy chips. They tasted like the chewed-up paper and spit we used to shoot through hollowed-out pens at school.

'It's a pity. He's cute! And a complete lack of morals, too...' Rock seemed lost for a moment, and I leaned over the table to wipe some of the grease from his face. 'So you're going to dump him?'

'Yeah! He's officially dumped.'

'Good for you. Can I have his number?'

'Only if you pay for my meal.'

'Deal!'

77. What makes my eyes blue

We threw bits of our designer sandwiches to the ducks in Stephen's Green.

'Why are you gay?' Khalid asked.

'What do you mean, *why* am I gay?'

'Well, why do you think you're gay?'

'I don't *think* I'm gay. I just am.'

'But what makes you gay?'

'Nothing *makes* me gay. That's like saying, what makes my eyes blue?'

A crowd of Spaniards chattered past, oblivious to the sun, huddling over cigarettes.

'You mean – genetics?'

'Bullshit. My eyes are blue because they *look* blue to you. They're colourless to me. The world isn't blue just because I see through blue eyes.'

The male ducks gang-raped a squawking female.

'You get blue sometimes.'

'Yeah. Only over you, though.'

78. A gratuitous shot of Daniel's damn fine ass

Daniel and I first met on a filmset for a Disney movie. The elves they hired couldn't do the Elf Dance with convincing chirp and cheer, so we got drafted in to supply instant camp. Despite the glue-on ears, rosy cheeks, pointy hats and stripy tights, Daniel looked *cute*. He just had *it*, the take-him-home-to-mommy factor, and when he asked me to tie his sash tighter round his ass, I thought, *Ker-ching! Gay as a Christmas Elf!* He struck up a conversation about his boyband, and how they were cool, but not cool enough – and I looked the part, did I want to audition?

I thought it was a really schmaltzy chat-up line, so of course I kept in touch. We made a couple of dates to talk shit about the band and its progression, so when the real and actual auditions happened – *like, huh?* – me and Decko aced them cos we knew exactly what they wanted.

Bam! It was a long, hard slog to the bottom of the pile.

I mean, 'It's hard work, but it's fun!'

See, Daniel is perfect cos he's so innocent, so totally uncynical. He lost two stone, he fixed his hair, he never drinks, he doesn't do carbs, and when he smiles, you just want to hug him. He's a perfect pop star!

It's a pity he's straight. He's got a damn fine ass.

So we took Daniel out for a drink. The lads all fell in love, though no one could remember what our band was supposed to be called.

'Poppers?'

'The Picnickers?'

'We're called Package! Go out and buy us before two of our livers die in obscurity and Daniel becomes a global megastar!'

'Daniel, sweetie! Did you see in the paper that your former dance teacher was nearly hit by the LUAS?' Terry carries round a copy of the news story so he can read it in hilarious detail to anyone who knows the poor chap.

'Yeah, I saw that,' Daniel said, all concerned. 'He was on his bike ...'

'Sweetie, don't you believe it! *I* heard he was lying on the tracks with his legs in the air!'

Daniel grinned sheepishly. I love that guy! I deserve to fail cos he's such a fucking *pro*.

My life was becoming more and more like a rubbish ballad. If you're a romantic, you might enjoy the heartbreak that Khalid and I were destined for. Otherwise, you might just want to linger on Daniel's damn fine ass for a little while longer.

79. Disco bitching

'Excuse me! Excuse me, mister!' A titty blonde in a white boob-tube staggered up and clutched my arm.

'Howaya.'

'Yeh don't mind me asking, do yeh, but are yeh *gay*?'

'Well, yeah, I am actually.'

'Oh! Are yeh really? Cos me and the girls here,' she pointed to her friends, who leered, 'we were just saying, doesn't he look really *gay* in that top?'

'That's me. Gay.'

'Well! Fair play to yeh!'

'And – you don't mind me asking – are you a natural blonde?'

'I am indeed, yeah!' She teased her golden tresses.

'Well! Fair play to yeh!'

She was well chuffed, the silly moo.

80. Hangin' with my homos

My phone vibrated in my pocket. It was a message from Khalid.

'Sweetie! Shove it up your arse – it's the closest you'll ever get!'

> **WHAT'S DA WORD,**
> **NIGGA ? WE IS IN**
> **DA Q-BAR, COME**
> **ON JOIN US !**
> **Options**

I went. Everyone else had more sense and stayed to have a good goss about what a dope I was, I hope. I kissed Daniel goodbye and got a peck on the cheek in return, for good luck.

I queued for ages with a pack of mingers. I could see the gang inside, and they waved – Khalid, a girl, Jen, her fella, his mates, and some random arty-student types, who looked as uncomfortable as I felt in the shivering conga-line of humanity's style-forsaken dregs, but at least *they* had rudely named cocktails to hide behind.

After getting past the tuxedoed apes, I met the gang and got introduced, inevitably, to Khalid's girlfriend.

'This is Alison, this is Anto. You're side by side in my phone, so you should get on great!'

Alison smiled frostily, which she did really well, cos she was gorgeous (of course).

'Khalid,' I said, 'do me a favour and buy me a really expensive fuck-off cocktail.'

'Which one?'

'The biggest, most fuck-off one, please.'

'OK. You da man!'

I tried to have a chat with Alison, but it was like stabbing yourself in the face with an ice-pick.

Jen came to rescue me just as Khalid plonked a satisfyingly huge cocktail in my hands.

'Are you chatting up my girlfriend?'

'Which one?'

'I can't tell,' he said, eyes closed and sniffing the air. 'They both smell of the perfume I always buy my bitches!'

They both looked ready to murder us, so I threw back the cocktail, thrust the empty glass at Khalid and, grabbing Jen and Alison with either hand, stormed onto the dancefloor. For once I was leaving Jen's fella alone and by the time I'd dirty-danced with Alison, we were all having what could pass for a civilized night. We all smiled, and no one drew blood. Success!

Khalid made a beeline for me when I hit the bar.

'Good man, Khalid, get me another.'

'Alright.'

'Your girlfriend's gorgeous. Well done you! You must be delighted.'

All around us, fat old men were buying champagne for young girls, who were giggling to their faces and laughing behind their backs.

'I'll be honest,' Khalid said, plonking another fuck-off cocktail in front of me and popping the cherry from his into his mouth. 'The only thing wrong with Alison is – she hasn't got a penis!'

'No problem,' I said. 'I'll buy her a strap-on for your birthday.'

Jen appeared at my shoulder and tugged at my elbow. 'Alison's *raging* you're talking to him, come on!' She didn't bother to keep her voice down so Khalid wouldn't hear.

'Duty calls,' I said. 'I'm dancing with Jen. You better get back to your gorgeous girlfriend.'

'She *is* gorgeous,' he said seriously, and Jen stopped tugging at my arm. 'But you know ...' he paused to drain his drink, 'I'd rather take you home, Anto.'

'Anto wouldn't go with you if you were the last bit of rough on the planet!' Jen said hotly. Khalid laughed as Jen and I melted into the throng of dancers – probably because he knew she was wrong.

81. The coffee blues

'Sweetie,' Terry said with a sigh, and I knew a little anecdote-and-observation was on the way. I sugared my double espresso (twice) as Terry continued.

'You know those gloomy mornings when you just can't get out of bed? You haven't slept because you've stayed over in your man's place on a week night, so you're grumpy because you both got too drunk for sex, and now Peter's alarm clock has gone off early and you're in much too bad form to be frisky ... *well*, that was this morning, and sweetie, I *know* I look hideous, but I couldn't be arsed even doing my hair. I just looked at my *bags* in the mirror and said *fuck* it. You think you're saving time and effort, but it's a false economy, because by the time you get to work, *you* know that *everyone else* knows you're a dirty stop-out and a lazy ho.'

I stirred my coffee and nodded sympathetically. The traumatically unglamorous nature of work should not be lightly dismissed.

'But that's not the worst of it! I went to get my daily latte in the bijou Coffee Society we have in the IFSC, and of *course* the guy who works there is so *fit* – he's an icon, sweetie – and his *hair*!'

Terry put his coffee down, shook his head, and shrugged.

'I think to myself – Sweetie, you've got the suit, you work for the bank, he's serving you your coffee – but at the end of the day, he's got *good hair*. Do you know what I mean?'

The tedium of a working day never fails to gnaw at your fabulous self-image.

'I'm afraid he wins,' I said.

'Exactly, sweetie, exactly.'

Terry's untamed locks glistened as he supped his coffee, stray curls tumbling like weeds around his ears. They only needed a *little* grooming ...

I drank my double espresso in one gulp. You get used to the taste – the nicotine-sour tang, like the dregs in a cowboy's corner-dwelling spittoon.

82. Gloom Twinkies

Amid fat-assed American tourists and pan-European revellers, Gloom Twinkies roam Temple Bar. They wear black, they scowl, they hang around corners in clumps of hormonal disgruntlement. His mating call is the guffaw; hers the high-pitched squeal. Their god is Kurt Cobain – their first memory of him is when he blew his head off, sealing his unimpeachably mythic status. Their dads are mostly lawyers, doctors and businessmen. They drink cider, and fruit liqueurs robbed off their mums, whom they're unembarrassed to be seen shopping with in Corporate Anti-Corporate skateboard boutiques, because she foots the bill. They wear piercings and tattoos and think this means something. They argue about shit American Pop Anti-Pop guitar bands. They are the Irish faction of a global breed of uniformed Cool Anti-Cool. They are © Angst Inc.

They all want to be rich and, unlike previous generations of ambitious outsiders, they are proud to admit it, because that is not selling out, that is winning.

83. The sting

The sun shone like a sweaty fried egg, dripping grease over strings of shoppers, sizzling like sausages up and down Grafton Street. As we traipsed towards Stephen's Green, I mouthed off about Khalid because, of course, you can't help talking about the people you love, hate, are obsessed with, worship, despise, change your mind about all the time. I was telling the lads about the how-do-you-know-you're-gay conversation as an afterthought to the Q-Bar nonsense, and I'd worked myself up to being pretty pissed off – so when I tripped over Cathal fucking Woods in the park, I was in no mood for his drunken misery.

'Are you *still* drinking?' I fired at him.

He looked round at all his mates, who sniggered.

'Your wife's here, Cathal!'

'Hehehe!'

'I hope you choke on your own vomit,' I said. 'I know you'd rather choke on my cock and instead you're just boozing yourself into oblivion, getting chucked off the team, getting fucking *fat* when you used to be gorgeous –'

His mates gawped, Jaysus-ed, and my mates stirred uneasily beside me. Cathal's fist closed tighter round his can.

'– and wasting your fucking life playing it straight. You're pathetic. You're a closet-case loser and you're in my fucking *way*.'

I kicked a path through their litter of cans, both warm and full and crushed and empty, and Cathal yelled after me, some generic abuse I can't even remember. His mates' jeers (at him or at me?) followed his can, squashed in rage and still half-full, as it whacked off my back, splashing me with beer froth.

'You fucking *eejit*, Anto.'

'They're fucking *raging*.'

'Let's get out of here, seriously.'

'Fuck them,' I said, throwing Cathal the finger over my shoulder, where a ripe new bruise was swelling, aching like a love-bite.

84. Blacks in the jacks

In the club, as usual, you couldn't go for a piss without having to tip the black guy handing you sheets of paper to dry your hands on – or just standing there, watching you piss. Why? Are we supposed to be intimidated into tipping by his blackness? It's such a shitty job I usually tip, but I think I shouldn't. It's so not classy, for anyone involved.

Some loudmouth earnest piss-head was lecturing the toilet attendant on slave and immigrant history – *quelle* eek!

'And, right, in forty years, like, two generations, you'll all have blended in, and, and, there'll be no racism, though it's hard *now*, I know, no one will care, and, like, the Irish have emigrated all over the world, and, like, it was *No Blacks, No Irish*, you know, and, man, we're all the same …'

The black guy stood there nodding – what was he supposed to do? – probably wishing your man would shut up and show some solidarity with a big fat tip, ('But, loike, would that be, loike, a *collusion* with colonialism?')

Yadda, yadda.

'Get your soap and get off your soap-box,' someone said. I snuck out without tipping – hehe! – thinking of something Khalid once said:

'Every time I go to a bar or a club here, and there's people who are black, or just not white, I always talk to them. As if we've got anything in common! That's pretty racist, isn't it?'

I said I always avoided other gay guys in straight bars in case they thought I was a desperate closet case – which wasn't much better, really.

85. Kissing with his fists

I stumbled out of the club. Light crystallized in pinpoints, like seeing stars before you faint. I was totally fucked. The lads were inside but I was so totally fucked I left early, alone.

Mistake.

I swayed down the alley for a piss. One-to-one pint-to-piss ratio. Bad sign. I realized I was pointing my splashy cock at a shoe. It wasn't mine. I shook my cock dry. I shook my face to clear the picture, but someone said, 'I think the faggot just pissed on your Reeboks, Cathal.'

'Unh,' I said. And then the first punch came.

I fell to the ground. It happened as quickly as falling in love. I barely had time to feel pain, my hands between my legs, my body tensed as if I was about to come. The heavy thuds, as if someone was kicking a ball against a wall one street away. Someone puked. It splattered on my face.

I struck out. The one who was kicking me – Cathal – fell on me, tangled up in my legs. A cop car flashed blue, squealed. The others ran. I grabbed Cathal by the throat – his face white, hands flailing, eyes as wide as road-kill – and I kissed him deeply in the mouth.

Footfalls.

He gasped for air.

I folded up on myself, spent, and let the dizzy lights burn out, like fireflies fucking on the last day of summer.

86. Getting cosy on the couch

I soon sobered up when I came to – from the shock, I suppose. The cops dropped me home – my *real* home – after they took my statement. Yes, it was a 'known' gay bar. No, I didn't know my assailants. No, they didn't 'entice' me into the alleyway, I was having a piss if they wanted to go sniff the ground – no, I hadn't been robbed. Yes, I would be more careful in future. No, of course not, how could I expect them to chase the assailants, bla bla bla …

I didn't expect *anything* from the cops. I suppose I blamed myself for humiliating Cathal. I could still taste my blood mingled with the sweaty sheen of beer from his lips. Had I imagined the slide of his tongue on mine? The startled sigh as he closed his eyes?

My head hurt.

There was no sign of Cathal and his cronies at our flats, worse luck. I would've shopped them to the cops if they'd been hanging around waiting to get arrested, but I wasn't going to *report* them. I'd be beaten to a pulp twice more before breakfast if I did.

I found Ma and Cathy on the sofa watching *Buffy*. Ma was wearing Cathy's rugby top and Cathy was wearing Ma's furry slippers. I stood for a while, drinking in the female chit-chat, the cosy room that had never looked so homely, the comfort of just having somewhere to curl up and hurt. The women fairly shrieked when they saw me – 'We weren't expecting you! Well, sit down and hear the camogie scandal – Jesus! Anto, your face! What happ – Who was it? Get him a cloth for his eye, oh, it's a shiner!'

I succumbed to their fussing. Ma dabbed moisturizer all over my face – I don't know why.

'It's wonderful, you'll feel better, it's for *sensitive* skin.'

Cathy pottered in and out, fixing cushions and making tea as if she owned the place.

'Ma, I don't *have* sensitive skin,' I moaned, twisting around like a kid as she daubed me with hypoallergenic cold cream.

'Nonsense! You're *very* sensitive. How else would you go and get yourself beaten up? Oh, I'll murder them! Tell us who they were and your da will *break* them!'

'I might be sensitive, but my skin is dead thick. Which is a good job around here,' I muttered. 'Ow!'

Cathy had it all sorted out before I had time to hog the sofa for a good night's snooze. 'I rang Khalid!' she trilled. 'He's picking you up here tomorrow morning to walk you to work. I tried to ring Decko but I couldn't get through. Now, as your medical adviser, get some hot, sugary tea for the shock – here you go – and I'll put your poor mum to bed, she's in a worse state than you!'

Ma kissed me goodnight, turned off the light, and succumbed to Cathy's promise to put her to bed. I lay on the sofa, too awake. Alcohol and memories bubbled in my brain – Khalid's words, Cathal's looks, the salty kiss of promises, broken.

My old home – it was *still* my home – slumbered all around me. I let it gently tug me into restless sleep.

87. Solidarity

I was woken up by Khalid tickling my feet.

'Hello, rude-boy! How are you feeling?'

'Groggy.' I picked the eye-snot out of my lashes. Cathy came floating in from the kitchen, trailing crumbs of toast and a dazzling smile.

'Khalid!'

'Hello, rude-girl. You look lovely. What are you doing here?'

She ignored the question, the toast suspended halfway to her mouth.

'What have you done to your face?'

Khalid had a smudgy ring of eyeliner around one eye.

'What do you mean?'

'It's all black.'

'Is it cos I is black?' he asked solemnly.

'No, it isn't! You're not black, you're brown. And you've got make-up all over your face!'

It hit me for the first time that wanking on about Khalid's *golden* skin was a bit like saying, 'You're not gay, you're miserable.'

'I'm wearing a black eye in solidarity with my nigger, Anto.'

'Hmmm ... I don't know who's worse ...'

'Where is everyone?' I piped up. 'Where's my *actual* family?'

'Your mum's in the shower – she's had a long night. Your dad and Zak are at the football tournament, of course. Didn't you know?'

'No.'

'Well, they are, so your mum had some time to herself for a change! Eat your breakfast, you're going to be late. And you can't have the day off, it's best to keep to your routine!'

Khalid walked me towards work, even though he didn't have to. I explained about Cathal, but I didn't say that I'd kissed him. I didn't want Khalid to think that I still *liked* Cathal, or anything.

The whole time we were walking, talking shit, I was thinking, *Yeah ... you're a mate. But it's guys like me who take the beatings for closet cases like you.*

88. Lazy little freckles

I didn't bother going to work. We sat by the river and threw sticks into the sluggish current. It was bilious and brown, hairy with weeds and slimy with wet, spongy effluent. Cars slid smoothly in one direction, towards the glittering, mirrored buildings, as if the industrial estate was drawing breath and sucking little tin plankton into its drowning lungs.

My phone rang.

'Anto! Guess what?'

'What?'

'Guess!'

'Eh, Cathal Woods has committed an honourable suicide by disembowelling himself into a urinal. It's Emily,' I said to Khalid.

'What? No! What's he got to – no, it's about *me*.'

'You're pregnant?'

'Do I *sound* pregnant?'

'You've, I dunno, you've killed Trev?'

'I'm getting married!'

'To Trev?'

'No, Trev is a dead loss. I've got a new man, he's called Dean, and he's crazy about me! We're engaged!'

'You're nuts.'

'Yeah, but so what? Will you be my bridesmaid?'

'No.'

'I was going to dress you up in gold and have you throwing rose petals up the aisle in front of me. Or you could be Cupid – will you wear a nappy?'

'No! I hate weddings! She says she's getting *married*,' I said to Khalid.

'Spoilsport!' Emily said cheerfully. 'Don't tell Ma. I'm not getting hitched just *yet*. Right, I'm going, I have to ring Lara and make sure my wedding's before hers, haha!'

Emily rang off and Khalid scratched his tummy, letting his T-shirt lift just enough to catch a glimpse of the track of fine hair climbing to his belly-button.

'Let's celebrate,' he said. 'A bottle of wine, some blow … some blow-back, it'll be cool.'

Sun dappled our hairy arms.

'My freckles are darker than your skin.'

'You're my nigger, man. We'll get some milkshakes too.'

'Cool.'

We trawled through the bleached grass and faded litter, the motorway gleaming like a mirage in the desert. We walked like a time-lapse movie shot beside the zipping cars, thinking of the good shit we could cram our bodies full of. Our freckles glittered in the cool morning sunshine.

89. So cool, you're cold

'Sometimes, you're so cool, you're cold,' he said.

I lit another cigarette.

'You've got everything. You're cute, you're funny, you're rude. You could have anyone you wanted!'

Except you, I thought. *Isn't that what I'm supposed to think?*

His eyes watered from the smoke.

'Take your shoes and socks off. Come on,' I said.

'My feet are a bit smelly.'

'So wash them, you tramp. Stick them in the sink and give them a soaping.'

While he was gone, I read my horoscope for the week.

SCORPIO 24 OCT.–21 NOV.

Battle stations on the home front! Old rivalries are rearing their heads, and you're in danger of lashing out under pressure, in true Scorpio style. Try not to hurt the ones you love. If it feels like they're hurting you – well, isn't that the price you pay for being the Zodiac's most passionate creature? Take a deep breath. With Jupiter on the horizon, goodwill flourishes once the stormclouds have lifted.

He came back from the bathroom leaving a trail of damp footprints all the way. 'What does your horoscope say?'

'The usual. *Things are a bit shit now, but hang on in there – they'll get better!*'

He lay across the sofa and I dried his feet with Decko's good towel. The soles of his feet were pale, his toes long and wriggly.

'Do you shave these bits of your feet?' I wondered out loud, tracing the stems where his toes crept into his fuzzy ankle.

'Don't have to. I'm not really hairy – you're more hairy than me, and you're gay.'

I gave him a look.

'You know, if you look in all those gay mags, all the men are really muscley and smooth. How come you're not rock-hard handsome?'

I smacked his feet.

'I always wish I was gay when I read those mags. I'd be gorgeous.'

'Sit still.'

I painted his toenails metallic blue. My cigarette burned out in the ashtray, a dead grey worm, like the worms I imagined would claim cancer victims in the grave.

'How come you don't have another boyfriend yet?'

I shrugged.

'I worry about you.'

'Don't bother.'

'Come here.'

'I *am* here.'

'No. Closer.'

I looked up into his earnest face.

'Here,' he said, patting his knees. 'I've something to tell you.'

'Go on.'

'It's ... personal.'

He waited, but I said nothing.

'Ever since ... Jennifer, I haven't liked anyone in ages. But then ... then there's ... it's sort of complicated.'

He turned his face to the floor, shunting his lips like a retard as he struggled for the words.

'Why? Why is it complicated?'

'It would – I'd have to change –'

'Is it because of this – other person?'

'It's cos – well, this other person – there's lots of reasons, but, like, for starters, this ... person is a relative of Jennifer's.'

'Right.'

He put his hands on my knees and looked me straight in the eye.

'You promise not to – say anything?'

'You haven't done anything. Yet.'

'Yeah.' He sighed. 'At your party ... I realized ...'

'What?'

'There's only one person since Jennifer.'

He took a deep breath. He blinked. Then he deflated, jerked his hands from my body.

'It's Emily,' he said.

It was like a punch to the mouth.

'I kissed Emily at your party –'

'You *bastard.*'

'I got carried away!'

'Fuck off –'

'*She* kissed *me!*'

'Why are you *telling* me this?'

'I needed to talk about it –'

'You are *so* full of shit.'

He tried to grab my arm as I clambered out from between his legs. I pushed him off me. He tumbled to the floor, headfirst, his painted toes flashing like bullets as he fell.

I hope he breaks his fucking neck, I thought, but only for a second. I couldn't stay mad at the hurt and confusion in his eyes.

I sent him to the Spar up our road so I could calm down. While he was gone, I threw the magazine with my horoscope in the bin.

I'd had enough of magic. I wanted *reality*.

He returned, still a bit dazed, and we drank the rest of the wine with the chocolate he'd bought. He took the length of the sofa. I refused to be drawn, tucking myself up in an armchair.

I let him bullshit me some more about Emily. The whole time, I imagined that he'd fractured his skull in the fall. I saw the slow suffusion of blood in his brain, the flowering of unconscious thoughts as they leaked from his head. Would he slip to the floor, love bruising his eyes? Would he die at my feet, his tears ruining the suede trainers I'd kept in the divorce from Chris?

As he talked on, I stopped listening. I watched the red wine saturate his lips, and felt the same red wine saturate my heart.

90. How we unfurl and seem to disappear

We lay in a haze of smoke, face-to-face and upside-down to each other.

'I can't believe Emily's getting married. At least, I can *believe* it, I wouldn't put *any*thing past her. She never had any taste.'

'It's very sudden.'

'Why do girls do that? Why do they need to get married? I bet he's a bollix.'

'I don't want to get married.'

'Good.'

'I probably will though ... eventually.'

I took a deep draw and held it in. Khalid closed his eyes. I blew smoke, like a burst pillow of down, into his face.

'You probably will,' I said.

'It's just what you do.'

'Sure.'

'Don't you ever want to get married? To a bloke, I mean.'

'No. I don't know.'

'If you were allowed to. You can in some places. I read about it in *GCN*.'

'You read *GCN*?'

Khalid laughed. 'My dad and my other brother, Rick – Tariq, you know? – took me out for dinner when they were over here in Dublin, and I read *GCN* at the dinner table! My dad hadn't a clue. Rick wasn't too happy.'

'I bet.'

'But wouldn't you marry the right guy?'

'I suppose. If it meant tax breaks.'

'What about kids?'

'No way.'

'Why not?'

'There's already too many. It's just vanity, and the moral superiority of breeders. *We perpetuate the human race therefore we are better than you.* What a joke. As if they breed for *humanity*, and not just so someone can wipe their arses when they're too old.'

'I like kids. They're so funny.'

'And then they inevitably grow up to be wankers like their parents.'

'No harm trying.'

'I have enough trouble trying to be perfect *myself*. I wouldn't breed till *I* was perfect. Then I could worry about creating little cool people.'

'You'd be a good father.'

'Ah, stop. How's Alison?'

'She's alright. She likes my credit card.'

'Can you afford her?'

'Yeah. She'll do. My family have stopped asking awkward questions!'

I held the joint to his mouth. He groaned.

'I hate weddings. I'll be on my own, surrounded by breeders.'

'You can take a mate.'

'Nope.'

'Why not?'

'I'd take my fella, if I had one. But I'm not taking a mate, just to not be alone.'

'You should take me.'

'Yeah, right.'

'You should! It'd be brilliant. Will you take me to Emily's wedding?'

'Why? So you can eye up my sisters all night?'

'No,' he said, seriously. 'I shouldn't – I don't want to talk about that. Forget Emily, I don't want to *think* about your sisters, I –'

'You're rambling.'

Khalid sighed and sank back into the carpet. 'I think we'd have a laugh, that's all. We always have a laugh, until …'

'Yeah. Until.'

We said nothing for a while. The roach began to burn my fingertips.

'It's a bad idea,' I said finally.

'The wedding mightn't even happen,' Khalid muttered. 'Or it mightn't even happen for *ages*. You could at least pretend you wanted to take me.'

'It's just a bad idea,' I said. 'You're *not* my fella and I'm not taking you to any wedding so you can pretend you *are* for a day.'

The joint burned out. We watched each other's mouths breathe, nostrils slightly heaving now and then. Our lazy eyes fluttered while our bodies lay flickering with static, unwinding at the edges, unravelling, then vanished.

Khalid's disembodied voice offered to fix my black eye with make-up.

I kind of liked it though. It was rough, it was sexy, it was a badge of pride. I decided to get a suedehead to match.

New hair, new Anto.

91. Tiny scars become sexy

Ma made me come home the next day, to make sure that I wasn't falling apart without her to make me soup. There was still no sign of Cathal skulking about, which was disappointing. I would have loved to stride past him looking bloodied but fucking cool, but he was probably crying over a can and looking at his lips in a mirror.

My suedehead showed off my scars. I have one from being flung from a go-kart when I was eight – I'd taken a corner too fast. The slice of naked skin right on my hairline looked like a deliberate nick with a razorblade. I also have a two-incher carved on my crown from when I collapsed after a Childline concert. I'd been too excited to eat. It's deadly!

'Lookin' tough, Anto!' Zak said. 'I like it.'

'Cheers. It's my macho look.'

'Yeah, right. You wanna look macho, you should borrow one of Ma's tracksuits!'

'No, ta. I'll stick to being pretty. What'd you do all day?'

'Ugh – I ran into some of those anti-whaddya-call-it protesters. Capple-something.'

'Anti-capitalist.'

'Yeah, them. What are they *at*? You can't take them serious, they look homeless. Pack of wretches.'

'I suppose they believe in what they do …'

'They're hippies!' Zak fairly spat the word into his Centra baguette. His face wrinkled in disgust, like a crumpled fiver. 'They have hair like rope and think that playing drums is gonna change the world. Smelly, sad, pathetic – ugh, I can't even describe them. *Losers.*' Munch, munch. 'They totally miss the point.'

'What's the point?'

'You gotta get up and get on with it,' Zak said promptly. 'If you don't like where you're at, get some money and *go*. And I don't mind getting Ma and Da outta here, but yous can all look after yourselves!' Then he turned to the sports page and thought no more about it.

It must be easy, being Zak.

'Anyway, what's up with you?' he asked, not looking up.

'Ah, nothing. Just thinking about this loser I like.'

'Forget him. Gets you nowhere, mooning after some fella. We're not worth it!'

'Yeah.'

'I hear you got beat up.'

'Yeah.'

'If you find out who it was I'll kick his fucking head in.'

'Thanks, Zak. But you're, like, nine stone of chewed chewing-gum.'

'I'm eight-and-a-half stone. So I'll *get* someone to do it.'

I wanted to say something blokey, to thank him properly, and laugh, and let him know that I was tough enough, even if I wasn't really. But I couldn't think of anything to say.

Da and Ma were in the kitchen, swapping G.A.A. stories from their few days apart. Ma kept automatically topping up Da's beer. I remembered the woman on the phone, the one who used to go drinking with her da, and I realized just how little I knew my own.

I knew that he didn't shave very well and always left jam on the butter-knife. I knew that his colour was too high and he resented paying the price of a pint for a haircut. I knew that he only got sentimental over Gaelic football. He hadn't even asked about my black eye, maybe because he knew how I got it.

'I'm having a girl's day out with some of the rugby geshas before the match,' Ma was saying. 'Remember Cathy? The pretty one?' Ma kept pouring, keeping the froth expertly under control. 'So you might want to look after the fellas. What d'you reckon?'

'Zak!' Da yelled. 'Are you coming to the final tomorrow?'

Zak opened his mouth, full of a mash of bread and egg and bacon and ketchup, and I said, 'I'll go.'

In the silence that followed, six eyes hit me.

I felt like my scars didn't look so tough any more.

92. Buds exploding in the sun

A child screamed. A second later, we flung ourselves at the window, bug-eyes glued to the pane. We broke away, a confused tangle, each of us running for the door, cramming through it and falling downstairs. Gary, Johnser, Moira all fell alongside us, spilling through the pissy concrete into the sharp slap of daylight. Fear etched the scene in hyper-reality.

Beyond the railings, cars and lorries crawled like creatures, drugged by the sun. Smog-stained buildings creaked like heroin teeth. The small strip of grass waltzed with butterflies. Toys grinned in the yard and, in the midst of them all, an old man tugged a baby from its brother's grasp.

The younger men leapt on the older one. He dropped the kid. The women rushed to the baby. Kicking, yelling, punching, the old man – Nilo, who'd been 'released into the community' two months ago – got what was coming to him.

The brothers' red hair glinted in the sickly sunshine. A couple of women scooped them off the ground, shielding the younger one from the sight of Nilo having his shit kicked in. The yells and the swearing drew more bums out of the towerblock, Cathal amongst them, running for his brothers, still dumb to the story unrolling around him. The women surrounded the Woods boys. Cathal caught a glimpse of Nilo sprawled on the tarmac. Someone's da dragged the old man off to where he could be beaten less publicly.

I stood there, not moving. Cathal had his youngest brother's hand. Zak stood back and Cathal, sick in the face, pushed roughly past without looking at me. Their Aunt Brenda cuddled the middle kid, Chris, in her beefy arms. He was crying, even though he was Zak's age. She scattered thanks and prayers around us all, offering Masses, and tea when the old bastard's every bone was broken.

We stood there, me and Zak and Johnser and Darren and Barry and I don't know who else, looking at the yard, feeling the way you feel when there's been a traffic accident ahead, and you've cheated death again, at someone else's expense. Partly small and random, but gloriously aware of the breeze on your bare face, the pulse of electricity flickering in your skin.

My da and the others eventually came round the corner, spitting on their hands and growling with self-congratulation. It seemed as good a time as any.

'Da,' I said, as the men humphed back inside the flats. 'Eh. Would you – would you like to go for a pint sometime?'

He didn't have to hesitate or think. His face split open like a ripe fruit. He just laughed.

93. Cocktails in the courtyard

I sat on the wall and swung my legs in the twinkling heat. Waves rose off the tarmac, rippling bricks and my body, as if the towerblock was seething with dope. Nilo had left a smattering of blood and one broken tooth behind. It glinted like a chip of marble kicked from someone's grave – a yellow and black stub, drizzled with red. His blood had splashed loudly on litter in one corner of the park, trailing with a whimper across the tarmac, glistening black like whispers on the ground. It soon would dry and be scuffed over, only gossip keeping its memory alive.

I waved to Mr McGinnity's twitching curtains. He joined me a few minutes later with two steaming cups of tea.

'Tea,' he said, 'is the only civilized thing to drink outside on a hot summer's day. I put a nip of whiskey in them.'

'Cheers.'

'So. What's the problem? Did seeing Nilo's blood on the pavement turn your poor little tummy?'

'Hardly. I mean, I suppose I feel sorry for him. But I would've felt sorrier for Séamus Woods.'

'Did Cathal give you that black eye?'

'Yeah.'

'Bastard,' Mr McG said briskly. 'Drink up your tea.'

I took a sip. You wouldn't think that tea laced with whiskey would hit the spot in a sweltering dead heat, but it did.

'Well,' Mr McG continued, 'now that Cathal's got *that* dose of violence out of his system, it'll be interesting to see what he turns to next.'

'What do you mean?'

'Look, darling, it's like this. Cathal is a repressed homosexual, so he took his rage and frustration out on you. It didn't work, of course. It never *does*. He'll feel even worse, probably because he likes you. Which means he'll either be very sorry – which I doubt – or he'll take it out on someone else. Maybe someone *you* like. Or, himself.'

'It would be kind of neat if he killed himself.'

'Oh, pooh. You don't mean that.'

'Maybe he'd leave a suicide note for my da, explaining his unrequited love for me and making my da see the error of his ways.'

'Oh, your *da*. Well, that's never going to happen. I'd advise you to drop your da from a height. You don't need his approval! He's hardly the target audience for your boyband, now is he?'

The common butterflies tumbled through the air like cellophane sweet-wrappers. Lorry fumes shimmered through girls' hair. Dogs bounced alongside push-prams, barking at traffic, crazy and stupid in the sun.

We swung our legs side by side, savouring the tea-and-whiskey cocktails, imagining all the things that might happen next.

We were pretty much wrong about everything, natch.

Before it got cold, Mr McG even rounded off the evening with a hug. 'I'm not your da, but I reckon I might make a good agony aunt!'

'Cheers!'

Then I went inside. The Woodses were still making tea for all the neighbours.

'The craic's ninety!' someone shouted. 'It's as good as a wake!'

Cathal watched me climb the stairs from his open doorway. His sad face glowed red, but whether it was from tears, or shame, or drink, I couldn't tell.

94. Belief

I can't shake the notion that the world, or humanity, or happiness, or truth, or beauty are really worth staying alive for. I'd like to be able to say, 'I believe in nothing,' but then, I don't disbelieve in anything either. Not strongly enough to bother topping myself on live TV during a national karaoke competition, or whatever. More true to say I don't care.

I quite like having money, but not enough to devote my life to earning it. And you can't believe in celebrity bullshit if you want to be famous – you have to see it as a game and play by the rules, believing only in yourself as a marketable commodity. It's such a bore, going through the motions. No wonder the Protestants decided everything was preordained and no amount of effort could earn you heaven or hell – it meant you could enjoy being yourself without all that tiresome Catholic guilt. Still, when I get the feeling that everyone else on the planet has been put here to populate my life story, I realize how much the world needs me. I'm all give, give, give!

Belief, though. Belief is dangerous. Look what happens when people follow through their beliefs to a logical conclusion. Ordinary madnesses – choosing profit over human safety; blowing up civilians in the name of whatever god you've been taught to fear; placing your faith and happiness in the hands and heart of one other person who's as flawed as you are.

If you have to choose one song to play at a party, make it Madonna. And if I have to choose one thing to believe in, I'm going to invest in one of her universal pop clichés, and choose the power of love – to touch another person's inner sadness, illuminate it, and let it burn out briefly with a kiss.

95. G.A.A.Y

Don't even ask about the final, cos I don't care. For the record, it was Khalid's team versus my da's, and my da's team was going to win, despite Khalid's mastery in the opening half of the match. I didn't care about the sweaty guys in shorts, or my da wailing like a banshee on the sidelines, or the crowds in scarves and flags and those woollen plaited two-tone head-bands – if you need any more proof that straights have no style, look no further than his'n'hers, XXL, day'n'nite *sportswear*. We even took separate sets of tickets, seats for the ladies and standing for the lads, as if we were in church a hundred years ago.

The wind whipped our asses up in the stands. I almost wished I was wearing an anorak like everyone else, but I'd thought I might use the time to work on my tan, so I was in a vest-top.

I sipped a Coke and nibbled on a rancid hot-dog while Zak filled me in on Cathal's brother's latest scam for getting the edge on the man he's marking in any match.

'What he does, right, is when the guy goes to shake his hand before the match – or give him the shoulder, if he's doing it right – *Ah, ref, ya fuckin' wanker!* – is, right, he grabs him by the balls and gives him a wink! *Free out, ya blind bastard!* Then the guy he's marking stays well clear for the whole match, hehehe!'

'This hot-dog's only half cooked. It's *tumescent*. It's got, like, a semi-hard-on. So, doesn't Chris get battered for that?'

'Nah. It's funny. I must try it!'

'There's safer places than the football pitch. I must take you to The George. You've even got a gay tan!'

'I didn't know it was Jen's bronzer! I though it was after-sun!'

'Yeah, right.'

Then there was lots of boring running and chasing and booting and cheering, until Khalid stopped halfway through dribbling the ball up the length of the pitch and broke into a mad dash towards the subs' bench.

'What the fuck is he *at*?' Zak yelped.

Then the crowd stood as one as Khalid landed an off-pitch tackle on the gleaming red head of Cathal Woods. Splat!

Flat on his back, pinned to the ground, a fist raised – ooh, and Cathal spun him over, tousling, ragged and rolling on the turf, doggy-style, like two little mongrels fighting over – me?

Now that's entertainment!

It was over too soon. Some wretched official who wouldn't know sport if it fucked him up the arse pulled them apart. Red card for Khalid; a stretcher for Cathal!

Woohoo!

'What was *that* about?' Zak asked, mystified. 'Kashani jeopardized the match, the bollix.'

'Back in a mo,' I lied. I legged it through the crush of bodies and all the commotion, down through the stalls, hoping to catch Khalid before he got to the changing rooms. Footsteps rang in the concrete tunnel – physios jogged past with the stretched-out, blanketed Cathal between them. He raised a hand at me with a grim little smile, and was gone. I just missed Khalid. I wasn't allowed in the changing room, of course.

'But I'm his mate!'

'I don't care if you're his fourth fucking wife, you're not getting in!'

I buggered off round by the back way to see if I could find Khalid showering beneath an open window, desperately in need of comfort, or a good lathering. A small army of cars were parked haphazardly in the grounds. I could see steam clouding up one tiny window – bingo!

And that was when I noticed one car – Da's car – rocking in the midst of all the other patient, stationary, empty vehicles. I hesitated.

Window, car, window, car …?

Someone's black hair humped up and down in the back seat. It *couldn't* be Khalid …

Da's furry dice leapt along to cute little muffled yelps. The car jiggled. Someone moaned, and someone else purred.

The dirty hallions!

I tiptoed over.

Stealthy. Quiet. Just a little peek…

I suppose I shouldn't have been *too* amazed to find my ma and Cathy going at it hell-for-leather.

96. Being alone

Sometimes it feels like the only moment that matters is the one when I will die. Everything that comes before is a rehearsal. That's why it doesn't matter if Khalid and I are together or not, we've had our time, and I should hug the moments to myself as comfort when I'm down.

You can't expect a happy ending, so I cling to small moments of happiness. I know this shouldn't be the point, but I cling because I'm scared to let go. I'm scared of being alone.

97. Lost in TV

'I haven't told anyone else,' I said, blowing smoke out the window.

'Fuck,' Decko said.

'You think I should casually mention that I saw them?'

'No! Jesus, I would *die*.'

The flowerbeds below were as neat and neutered as cute sushi lunches. I killed my cigarette on the concrete façade of our workplace and dropped the little cancer nebule into the grave perfection of a one-foot-square ashtray of plant-life, ruining its zen.

'Say nothing,' Decko said. 'It might have been a once off, or, or – an experiment.'

'Yeah, right.'

'I don't believe me either. Still, you'd hate to be outed by, erm, your own son. Or mate. Or anyone, really,' he continued, flustered. 'I mean, it's their decision what to do next. Oh my god, your poor da!'

'Oh, bla. It'll tighten him up. If he wasn't such a square, he could probably join in!'

'You do *not* mean that.'

'Nah. I'm putting a brave and camply cheerful face on my inner turmoil.'

'You should use this inner turmoil as an excuse to quit smoking.'

'Eh?'

'It's bad for our image.'

'I'll quit when we get our first hit single.'

'Ah, bullshit. We'll never get a hit single unless you quit smoking, how does that sound?'

'How about – we quit work? This vacuum of talent is sapping my will to live. I'll soon be bored beyond rebellion. Let's just get up and *go*.'

'Now?'

'Let's burn our headsets, overturn the water dispenser and set the computers to print out the lads' stash of Internet porn.'

'We could shit in the vegetarian lasagne on the way out.'

'That's the spirit.'

'We're going nowhere, aren't we?'

'Yeah.'

'Yeah.'

We sauntered back to the clock-in/clock-out machine, slipping our ID cards through its electronic snatch.

'Look,' Decko said awkwardly, 'if you want to, you know, talk about it ...'

'I don't,' I said quickly. 'Not yet, anyway.'

'Sure. Well. I'm here when you do.'

'I know. Thanks.'

It was a soap-opera moment, conducted entirely in *Coronation Street* accents. We giggled and sat at our adjacent, identical, blank-faced monitors. With what seemed like magic, but was really a complex retranslation of binary-coded data-input, our computers converted people and their lives into numbers, letters, tiny sub-particles of information, to be used or disposed of as deemed necessary to the smooth operation of a glitch-free, profitable existence. I envied them.

So I'd backed two losers in the coming-out race. My closest closet cases didn't need me; they'd found each other. I'd underestimated my women-folk, making me sexist as well as blind, stupid and more than a little bit lovesick.

98. Why I want to sing

Pop music should be simple, but it isn't easy. *You* try getting a global teen audience to fall at your feet in three minutes flat, then keeping them enthralled for long enough to flog millions of records, carve a niche in pop history and retire before the wrinkles kick in.

I want to sing so I can take the bad things in life – loneliness, breaking up, being a sap about some fella – and turn them into little gems of happiness. Yeah, it's Prozac. So what?

Pop recycles your emotions and puts you back on the dancefloor where you belong, ready to fall in love with some other beautiful loser, dancing for as long as you stay high, breaking your heart on the middle-eight, coming with every chorus and preparing to do it all over again – with every brand-new number-one hit, with every top-ten smash new entry, with every underground remix of a familiar tune – pulsating, merging, staying fresh. A happy-go-lucky disco bunny. Repeat to fade.

99. Auburn

Can I help it if I like my fellas coloured? It might sound weird – pervy, even – but I have such a crush on Ireland's indigenous minority of snoochy redheads. Is that wrong?

Chalk-white boys, sand-flecked with freckles. Green eyes blinking behind orange lashes, like the tricolour begging to be kissed. Or, like Cathal, cinnamon-skinned with auburn curls licking at his body like a gingerbread man sprung hot and ready from the oven.

Other people gag at the thought of red pubes, but to me, they're brittle slivers of golden love, kinky and flaming, outrageous for just existing so flamboyantly. Sure, there's an element of the exotic becoming erotic – so it's positive discrimination, and I'm racist!

I was sitting on my own in our swanky apartment, thinking about how your entire world can be reduced to the things you do and see and feel on a daily basis, dreaming of escape, when the stones began to bounce off the window.

Plip … plip … plip.

I ignored them, and they seemed to go away. Then a rock cracked against the pane, splintering the glass. The damage hung like a spiderweb trapped in morning dew. Swearing, I hopped across the room and looked down through the broken glass into the street. Cathal's red head burned like a halo. I elbowed the window, hard, and the glass fell like stars at his feet.

I poked my head out. Cathal squinted up at me.

'I'm coming down,' I said.

I legged it down the stairs.

Did he want to say sorry?

Did he want a scrap?

I opened the door. Cathal edged backwards, almost tripping down the steps.

'What?' I said.

He put his hand out. 'Shake?'

I looked at his hand – strong and blunt.

205

'OK.'

I took his hand. A little smile crept into the corners of his mouth. His eyes, cute as chocolate buttons, gleamed with mischief, as if the cheeky little gingerbread man was going to eat me.

Traffic slowed down. Broken glass crunched beneath our feet. I held my breath.

'Third time lucky,' he said.

100. Khalid speaks

Sometimes I said things that maybe I shouldn't have. Like when I took him shopping for lucky pants before we went clubbing in London. We went into Marks & Spencer's and I cornered the campest shop assistant I could find, and asked him loads of questions about which boxers fitted most snugly for the man who liked to stay in control of his tackle-and-ball-skills. He was all over me, and when he went to find my white, medium, hipster trunks, I turned to Anto and said, 'He's one of us!' I thought Anto would hop on that one, but he didn't.

Man! I was so nervous in those clubs. I kinda needed reassurance. That's why I stayed up talking all night, snuggling up beside Anto in bed. He didn't seem too bothered, which was cool.

I overdid it with Woodsy though. When I realized Ollie had put him back on the subs' bench, I saw red, and I ain't talking about his ginger afro. What he'd done just made me mad and I beat into him. I had my hand on his throat, and I said, 'Our love is worth more than your hate!' That was a bit much. Anyone coulda heard me!

In the shower, after I got the red card and lost the final, I was in a sorta daze. It was like, I dunno, I was tripping. I thought about Gaelic football, and how it was more about rough-and-tumble than soccer. I kinda missed soccer. It's more like dancing.

My perfect football match would go like this. We'd kit out and stream onto the pitch from opposite ends. We'd line up against our man, and we'd bow, and when the whistle blew, we'd take one another by the hand, and we'd waltz up and down and around the pitch for forty-five minutes a side, in clashing colours, with the entire stands full of orchestras playing. The goalies could be, like, Masters of Ceremony. We'd work a couple of tackles and fouls into the routine, as if we were playing against each other, but really we'd be supporting and complementing each other throughout the whole performance. We'd seem to fall, but pick each other up. We'd trip, and slide into one another's arms. We'd dip and dive and spring back into action, face-to-face, ballroom dancing in sweeps and circles on the turf.

It'd be beautiful.

So I decided that Anto deserved the truth. I got into a taxi, rehearsing what I was going to say, even though I always mess it up and wuss out whenever I do that.

From the top of his street, I saw Anto's window had been smashed in. Then I saw the tracksuit, and Cathal's red curls, and I thought, *Hold on, what's that fucker up to now?*

I told the taxi driver to slow down. Then Anto appeared at the door, and they squared up to each other. I was ready to jump out and pulverize Woodsy. Again. But they touched, and moved in for the kill, and I swear I nearly died when I saw what happened next. Cathal kissed Anto with his dirty mouth, and Anto kissed Cathal with his pink little tongue, and they stood on the doorstep, kissing, surrounded by broken glass and smiling passers-by and graffiti, and I thought, *Bad timing, mate! He's scored!*

I told the taxi driver to drive me home.

And I'm not going back to dance classes. You've got to teach yourself to dance.